TALES OF
TREACHERY

paradox
B O O K S

Pressname: Paradox Books

Copyright © 2014 Paradox Interactive AB

Authors: Lee Battersby, Luke Bean, Jordan Ellinger, James Erwin, Axel Kylander, Cory Lachance, James Mackie, M Harold Page, Aaron Rosenberg, Steven Savile, Anderson Scott, Joseph Sharp

Editor: Tomas Härenstam

Cover Art: Ola Larsson

ISBN: 978-91-87687-57-0

www.paradoxplaza.com/books

CONTENTS

INTRODUCTION

Paradox games have always embraced story-telling, and the new online landscape of social media, aggregation, and YouTube Let's Plays has helped people spread their stories around the world, allowing Paradox Development Studio to reach wider audiences and new heights of success.

The *Crusader Kings II* stories have always been a little bit different.

Though all of our strategy games sustain themselves through an evolving and emergent narrative born from the games' mechanics, the personal nature of *Crusader Kings II* sets it apart. You don't control a nation or an empire. You are not the gentle guiding hand of history. You are a bloodline and you control specific people at those specific moments when they have the power to change the course of history. You control their interactions, their relationships, and, often, their very souls.

A living world takes shape around you—a world that has villains and heroes, sinners and saints. The heir to your kingdom is not merely a set of numbers, but can be a stumbling block to harmony or a blessing to the future. Courtiers are plucked from obscurity to rule tiny counties, and you pray that a political marriage will turn into a love story. Through the course of the game, inheritance rules may mean that you could play both a king and that king's "evil brother" in succession.

Perhaps it is this forced empathy—this sense that every character you encounter has their own struggle and own motivations separate from yours—that makes *Crusader Kings II* such a durable and popular game for storytellers. Characters are cruel and will do cruel things, but you saw them tutored by an angry and envious soldier. What else could you expect?

It is not surprising, then, that this game more than any other in our stable has been a starting point for many of our fans to indulge the novelist that lies in almost every heart. Motives are ascribed, and back-stories are filled out, people become playwrights. Sometimes things are done in-game solely for dramatic purposes.

Tales of Treachery is an anthology of short stories inspired by players' experiences in *Crusader Kings II*. There are good guys and bad guys, and good girls and bad girls. There are mysteries and webs of intrigue. Court romance must compete against the sacred obligation to keep the lands united, and the Church is not a paper tiger.

We hope you enjoy what we have assembled here. And we hope it leads you back into another 500 hours of *Crusader Kings II*.

Troy Goodfellow
Assistant Developer
Paradox Interactive

THREE SACRIFICES
FOR THE LION

By M Harold Page

June 1314

Hundreds of English knights swept up the Stirling road. The summer sun flashed off burnished helmets and brought alive the merry colours of the surcoats and horse caparisons.

Robert de Bruce, King of Scots, watched them come and his sins weighed down his shoulders like a rain-soaked cloak. Behind him, his men passed jokes, yelled abuse at the oncoming English, or prayed too-loudly.

The English reached the far bank of the Bannock-burn. It wasn't much as streams went, but it had carved its own moat out of the fertile landscape. The warhorses half slid down the muddy side, dislodged great clods of earth into the shimmering water, then splashed across the stream bed, sending up white plumes.

3

"They'll not find the return journey quite so easy," said Kirkpatrick.

Robert grunted. He nudged Kipper—his Highland pony—into half turn so he could survey the two thousand or so lightly-armed Scots who waited on the edge of the New Park woods. They sat in the shade playing dice, or sprawled out on the pastureland, jack coats open, making the most of the sunshine. If God chose this moment to take His revenge, then they were all so many sacrificial lambs.

"No sign of archers, sire," said Kirkpatrick, his standard bearer.

"That's not what bothers me," said Robert.

"Ah well," said Kirkpatrick, leaning out from his saddle but not so much that the Lion banner dipped. He lowered his voice. "You do the fighting, Rob. Leave the judging to God."

Robert nodded. He straightened his back, savoured the familiar embrace of his mail, and raised his long-handled Gallowglass axe—a visible promise that he would join his men to fight on foot. "Form up under the trees! Let's give the English a Scottish welcome!"

Those who heard him raised a cheer. Kirkpatrick in his wake, Robert rode the length of the line and back repeating variations of the short speech. As he did, cheering men snatched up spears and axes. They scrambled over the shallow ditch and low bank to take their places under the canopy of leaves. As he'd hoped, the manoeuvre looked just enough like a retreat to fool the advancing English. As they got across the Bannockburn, clusters of knights broke away to race uphill, hooves kicking up clouds of dust from the dry summer grass.

"Earl of Hereford's forces, sire," said Kirkpatrick, all formal again.

Robert squinted into the glare. Sure enough, the banner of the de Bohun Earls of Hereford swayed high over the dust-shrouded column queueing to cross the burn. *Azure, a bend argent cotised or between six lions rampant or*; blue with a white stripe bracketed by golden lions rampant. "It *would* have to be lions."

Kirkpatrick's weather-worn face crumpled into a frown. "Sire?"

Robert looked back towards his men and beyond to where the rock of Stirling Castle dominated the landscape. The banner flying over the donjon tower was just a blurry little square against the blue sky, but he knew it sported English Leopards and not the Scottish Lion.

Not yet, at least…

July 1304 – Ten Years Earlier

A clunk resounded from the siege lines. The crowd on the edge of the camp fell silent as the huge trebuchet beam creaked upright like a tired soldier shouldering his spear.

Sir Robert de Bruce, Earl of Carrick, winced. His gaze flicked to the Lion of Scotland fluttering from the donjon tower of Stirling Castle. The stench of the English camp pressed in on him. He wanted to be out riding the hills, not watching King Edward smash the last fragment of Scottish resistance. But it was not his presence in the English army that made him a traitor. It was the fact he had submitted so readily to the foreign conqueror.

The trebuchet sling trailed out from the beam end, whipped over and unwrapped to hurl a carved stone ball high into the blue sky.

Beside Robert, Sir Harry de Bohun whooped and some of the younger English knights copied him.

Robert's stomach knotted. He glanced at Kirkpatrick. His cousin and marshal merely twitched a shoulder, hinting at a shrug.

The great stone passed over Stirling Castle's outer walls, arced down at the donjon, punched a black hole in its side. A heartbeat's delay, then the clap of the impact reached the crowd. They cheered as if watching a joust.

"Pretty damn impressive, eh Carrick?" said Sir Harry, teeth flashing, eyes boyishly wide despite the crinkle of laughter lines. "I can see why the king called it Warwolf!" Some of Robert's thoughts must have escaped onto his face because the veteran knight's expression sobered. "Oh sorry, Carrick, you must know some of the fellows in there."

Kirkpatrick gave Robert a warning glance, just a narrowing of the eyes.

Robert shook his head. "Not really, Sir Harry. They're all lesser folk." His gaze went back to the Lion banner.

Sir Harry patted his shoulder. "Never-the-less, it can't be easy, old man." His tone became confidential. "I've got some very nice Bordeaux red in my tent. Come by later and we can get utterly sozzled together."

"Ha!" Robert smiled. "Last time I was hungover for three days."

"And they say you Scots are tough!" Sir Harry looked past Robert. "Oh, here we go again."

The other war engines took their turn. Robert schooled his expression as man-powered trebuchets hurled clouds of fist-sized rocks into the castle's courtyard and rope-driven mangonels splintered the battered wooden hoardings that still clung to the wall-tops.

The air filled with crashes and thuds, and still the Lion banner flew from the donjon battlements.

An old man's voice said, "Sir Harry, I believe my lord Hereford is calling for you."

Both men turned and bowed to William Lamberton, Bishop of Saint Andrews.

Sir Harry recovered from an extravagant bow then set off through the throng of knights and nobles, slipping nimbly between knots of people, exchanging jokes, patting shoulders, bowing where appropriate, and always slightly deeper than he needed to.

The bishop and Robert exchanged grins.

"It's all a great game for him," said Robert.

"And yet one can't help but like him," said Lamberton. He drew closer and said conversationally, "The garrison say they fight for the Lion of Scotland."

"They certainly do not fight for any king," said Robert. "Though to be exact, they are not actually fighting." The garrison had tried to surrender three days earlier, but King Edward Longshanks had forced them back inside so he could demonstrate the War-wolf, specially shipped in from England and newly assembled.

"Yes, King Edward has an odd sense of humour," said the Bishop.

Kirkpatrick casually shifted position so as to hide the conversation from onlookers. He put his hands on his hips, making a barrier of himself.

"Oddly," said Robert, "the Scottish Lion seems both unperturbed by his laughter, and unmoved by the show of force."

Bishop Lamberton's eyes twinkled. He edged closer still. "We should talk, Carrick."

"Talk, my lord Bishop?" Robert leaned over to

speak in the old man's ear. "No, by St Mary, we should put things right."

June 1314

The Scots' spearmen—*Robert's* spearmen—dressed their lines amongst the trees of the hunting park. They formed a solid front, four ranks deep, bristling with points like a vast spiny caterpillar. There would be just enough overhead cover to blunt a Welsh arrow storm should it come, and the ditch and bank would take the edge off a cavalry charge—not that they should need it.

"What do you think, Kirkpatrick?" asked Robert.

Kirkpatrick shrugged his mailed shoulders. "If a bunch of town-bred weavers could stop the French at Courtrai, I think our lads should do just fine." His horse stamped nervously. "If God is with us, that is."

"There is that minor matter of their king being an excommunicate," said Robert. He nudged Kipper back around to face the oncoming enemy.

"God has already punished you," said Kirkpatrick. "Three brothers…"

Most of the Hereford's division was still the other side of the Bannockburn. However the more enthusiastic English knights who had got across now strung themselves out as the better mounted ones pulled ahead. They were decked in swathes of expensive fabric. Even so, enough armour showed through to make them look like unkillable men of iron.

Behind him, Bruce heard the chatter of the Scots die away so now the drum of the hooves carried through the air like thunderstorm coming in over distant mountains. "You know," he said, giving his axe a twirl to loosen his muscles, "Wallace once told me that his fight with the English started with a fishing expedition. I'm minded to follow his example."

Kirkpatrick drew his mount closer. "What are you doing, sire?"

Robert raised his voice so all would hear the order. "Kirkpatrick, keep the standard back near the trees." He pointed his axe for good measure. "I don't want a general charge. I'm going to find out if God is still angry with me."

"Sweet Jesus, Rob!" blurted Kirkpatrick. "At least get on a decent horse."

"Shush," said Robert. He patted his High lad pony. "Kipper thinks he's a destrier." He urged his mount downhill towards the advancing English knights, shaking off the summer heat as he picked up speed.

Kirkpatrick's voice came after him, "Robert. Don't do this."

February 1306 – Eight Years Earlier

A gust of wind plastered sleet into Robert's cloak so that it hung against his back like mail.

Kirkpatrick caught his arm. In the gathering dusk, his face was just a rumpled shadow under his hood. "Don't do this Robert."

"But I have to make things right," said Robert. He mounted the steps to the west door of the abbey church. "Let's get out of this foul weather, messirs."

Kirkpatrick nodded at Seton, Robert's brother-in-law, who did the office of page and slipped past to open one leaf of the double door. Sleet splattered over the threshold. Candlelight flared within.

Robert made to follow, but again Kirkpatrick caught his arm. He spoke loudly over the rising wind. "He once tried to choke you."

"Red Comyn is a great captain now," said Robert. "He's too old to be brawling in church."

Kirkpatrick shrugged. Hand on his sword, he entered the church. He glanced around. "Things are as agreed, lord," he said in the formal voice he reserved for when he was in public view as the Marshal of Robert's household.

Robert stepped into church with its wildly dancing candlelight. Behind him, Seton wrestled the door shut. The candles settled and Robert made out the three men who waited to his left, behind the columns of the north aisle. One had a luxuriant red beard that glowed like molten iron in the flame-lit gloom. However, Bruce would have recognised his hereditary foe even without the beard.

Red Comyn stood head and shoulders above his followers, like a bear crammed into courtly dress. He was equally formidable politically, having led the resistance to the English for years. Unfortunately, the Comyns and the Bruces were neighbours. Generations of jostling for land and power had made enemies of the families.

Robert led his companions up the south aisle. Just short of the crossing, he handed his sword and cloak to Seton.

Red Comyn met his eye, nodded.

The two of them stepped out of their respective aisles into the Nave proper and met before the rood screen. They clasped hands, Bruce trying not to flinch from the bigger man's grip, and exchanged a formal kiss. In silence, they passed under the rood screen's carved arch. Wet boots smacking the flagstones, they paced through the choir, treading the tombs of abbots and lords underfoot, and into the sanctuary.

Each man crossed himself before the altar then turned to face the other.

The wind rattled the stained glass windows. The candles on the altar flickered. Above them, Christ hung on his gilded cross, the dancing light making his ivory features writhe in pain.

Red Comyn's eyes twinkled, but he said nothing. It was up to Robert to start this conversation.

Robert coughed. "Thank you for meeting me, Comyn."

Red Comyn boomed, "I am always glad to talk to a fellow noble, Carrick." His great brows furrowed making his eyebrows arch like caterpillars. "Unless you have some conspiracy in mind, sir?"

Robert opened his mouth to deny the charge, but he would not perjure himself before the image of Christ. He opted instead for a truth. "Sir, I thought it time to end the old feud between our families."

"You have a nerve!" grated Red Comyn the way he had at Peebles just before trying to crush Robert's throat.

Robert held up his hands, a placatory gesture, but one that set up his defence if need be. "Your pardon, sir?"

"You *cannot* have those estates, Carrick," continued Red Comyn.

Robert blinked. "Estates, sir? By Saint Mary! What *are* you talking about?"

"Do not pretend you don't know what I am talking about, sir," boomed the red-bearded giant, pacing forward, great shoulders rising with his voice. "Your wife's grandfather murdered…*murdered*…my great great grandfather, his own brother, and those estates were a just weregild."

"Oh." Robert tried not to laugh. "Sweet Jesus, Comyn!"

"Ahem." Red Comyn glanced meaningfully at the altar.

Robert crossed himself. "I swear, Comyn, I did not come here seeking a few hides of Galloway hillside."

Red Comyn's spoke softly now, as if restraining himself. "Do you think this is a laughing matter, sir? Is murder a joke?"

"By my oath no, sir," said Robert. "We can draw up a document, I'll relinquish all claim to your land, whatever it is."

Red Comyn's shoulders dropped. His expression thawed. He grinned. "Oh well then, Carrick, the feud is over. The King's justices sit in the castle hall. We can go before them." He offered his arm. "Come sir."

Relief washed over Robert. He almost took the arm. Instead he said. "Wait, there is more."

Red Comyn's face became a mask. "Indeed?"

Robert shivered. He could see his breath steaming in the candlelight. It would be good to get back to his lodgings and a warm fire. "King Edward is old and ill," he said.

"That is true, Carrick," said Red Comyn. "Perhaps it is time King John returned from exile."

"Is that what we want, Comyn?" asked Bruce.

"Carrick?" Red Comyn drew himself up to his full height. "Are you saying that that mummery at Stracathro *meant* anything? They took his crown, but they could not undo his coronation. John de Balliol is our king and always will be."

Again, Bruce raised his hands. He took a step back from the red-bearded giant. "No, no, Comyn. It is just that Balliol is an old man too. Would he really want to leave his French estates?"

"You would not be insulting my uncle would you, sir?" said Red Comyn.

"Of course not, Comyn. But it seems…" Robert thought frantically "…a *harsh* thing to drag an old man from the comfort of retirement to face years of mud and blood."

Red Comyn nodded. "You're right, Bruce. When the time comes, we should proclaim his son as heir."

"Is this a time for an untested youth?" said Bruce. Now he had finally reached the part of the conversation for which he had prepared.

Red Comyn frowned but said nothing.

Robert pushed on. "King Edward has made peace with France."

"Indeed," said Red Comyn. "So no risk of Scottish knights being called off to foreign wars."

"Yes," said Robert. "But with France closed to them, where will ambitious English lords seek their fortunes? When the generous Edward of Caernarvon gains the throne, whose land will he be generous with?"

Red Comyn chuckled. "*Your* land perhaps, Bruce. I am better connected than you. I've fought the English since Dunbar—" He held out his big hands. A white scar like welt marred his left palm. "Here I am, in King Edward's favour, in possession of all my lands."

"Have you been to Wales, Comyn?" asked Robert. "Did you meet many native Welsh lords?"

Red Comyn's eyes narrowed. He shrugged. "We tried fighting the English. It did not go so well in the end."

"Better to fight an old leopard than a young one."

Red Comyn leaned closer, towering over Robert. "What are you saying, Carrick?"

Bruce stepped in. "Now's the time," said Robert.

"You are a hero of the war against the English, King John's nearest male relative—"

"—not counting his son."

"Not counting his son," agreed Robert. "Comyn, you must make yourself king and you must do it now."

Red Comyn threw back his head and laughed.

June 1314

The leading English knights swept uphill at the trot, dust billowing around them.

Bruce reined in Kipper. "We'll let him come to us."

Behind him, Kirkpatrick's yelled, "Come back here Rob! I've not kept you alive this long…" Robert could not look behind him. He had no way of knowing if his spearmen still stood under the trees, or if they had done the sensible thing instead and scattered off through the woods to make for home.

The summer air filled with the rolling thunder of hundreds of hooves drumming the dry earth as the enemy knights closed to within a bowshot.

Kipper's ears went back. Robert stroked his yellowy-brown hide. "We're old friends. Trust me."

Behind Robert, Kirkpatrick's cries died away. Robert closed his eyes and started to say a prayer. As always, the words wouldn't come. Instead, for a moment he was back in his youth with his brothers, listening to the storm coming up Carrick Vale, anticipating a mad ride home through the torrential rain, whooping and laughing.

Robert opened his eyes. Let God judge him on his deeds, not on some last moment pleading.

And, there was his mark, pulling ahead of the main body of English cavalry; a well-mounted knight in a fashionable visored helm, long lance held upright. It would dip shortly and then this trial-by-combat would begin.

Robert squinted into the glare. The fellow looked like one of the earl of Hereford's kin. Even better. He finally made out the shield: *Azure, a bend argent cotised argent between six lions rampant or;* a blue shield with a white stripe bracketed by golden lions rampant.

A stone settle in Robert's stomach. That red stripe broke the rule of tincture and caused some heralds to tut, but Sir Henry de Bohun just grinned at them.

Sir Henry de Bohun.

Sir Harry.

Greyer-haired now than he once was, but still as boyish as he was deadly with the lance. A good match for God's judgement, but Sir Harry probably thought the whole thing was a "jape" and that he'd chase Robert back to his lines and that they'd laugh over it together later once peace was made.

Robert whirled his Gallowglass axe one-handed and shouted, "Get back Harry! I don't want to kill you!"

Kipper sensed his mood. The little Highland pony reared and whinnied.

There was no way Sir Harry could hear him, but surely he must see the axe. Even so, his friend kept coming, the hooves of his great destrier kicking up clods of turf.

"Of course", murmured Robert. "He can no more back down than can I."

And now he did pray while Sir Harry's big destrier picked up its pace.

Kipper stamped and snuffled. Robert's mood was still affecting his mount. He inhaled slowly, then exhaled, expelling fear and feeling. This was a game to him now, not a rough and tumble tournament of the kind Sir Harry loved, but an earnest game of chess with each move setting up the next.

Behind Sir Harry, the other English knights reined in to the walk. King Edward might behave like a tyrannical Caesar—executing prisoners, keeping captive ladies in cages—but the young chivalry acted as if they were vying for a place at the Round Table. Robert knew they weren't going to interfere with the single combat. Even so, there would be time for just one pass before older, grimmer knights got across the burn.

Sir Harry's lanced dipped. He was making his final charge now.

Robert jiggled his arms making his mail rattle, shedding the tension in his muscles like a dog shaking off rainwater. He lifted the Gallowglass axe to his right shoulder, let go the reins and took the haft in both hands.

A familiar rushing sound filled Robert's ears. The rest of the world faded away leaving only the oncoming knight and the glinting lance tip. Though he came now at a full gallop, Sir Harry seemed to move as sluggishly as honey dripping from a wooden spoon on a winter's night.

Robert took another deep breath and exhaled. It was between him, his friend, and God himself.

February 1306

"King John Comyn?" The red bearded giant was still laughing. "Look how well that went for John Balliol! And I don't have nice French estates to hide in." His laughter died, like a door closing on an alehouse. "Did you see what happened to Wallace?" His fists balled. "*You're trying to destroy me!*"

Again, Robert raised his hands defensively. This was

too much like bear baiting. "No, I swear it. If you don't want to be king, then I'll do it. Have Carrick, sir. Hell, take Annandale as well if it will buy your support."

"Buy my support, sir?" boomed Red Comyn. "*Buy?*"

"Well then, sir, *you* be king. You're the one who trounced the English at Roslin. You're the one who went to ground with Wallace. You fought at Dunbar, and Falkirk…"

"At Falkirk," shot back Red Comyn, "you fought on the English side."

"That I did. Which is why it must be you."

Red Comyn stared down at Robert, eyes glittering in the candlelight. At length he asked, "How could this possibly work?"

"Did you see the Lion banner flying from the ramparts of Stirling Castle?" asked Robert. "The lesser folk will fight for the realm itself."

Red Comyn. "They did not do so well at Falkirk, though, against longbows and armoured knights."

Robert shrugged. "They followed where the nobles led, died where we submitted. Don't you feel some shame, Comyn?"

"They followed," said Red Comyn, "because it is right and proper that when a lord chooses to fight, his vassals follow him to war." He shot Robert a look of pure contempt. "Is this *it*? The great plan you wanted to share with me; go up against the best army in the West with a band of enthusiastic peasants? So this is why you made that pact with Bishop Lamberton."

Robert flinched. "What?"

"I have my spies." Red Comyn shrugged. "I wanted to take the measure of your grand scheme, but you have none, only a foolish commitment to rebellion. *Did you hear that uncle?*"

A man rose up from the choir stalls. "I did indeed." He shook himself, stamped his feet. "Cramped and cold down there," he said and Robert recognised Sir Robert Comyn, Red Comyn's uncle. He sidestepped along the stalls away from the sanctuary, a sword scabbard banging on the on his belt. "But worth the discomfort I'd say. Say, Red, do I get Carrick or Allendale?"

In a moment, Comyn's uncle would be free of the choir and blocking Robert's escape. Heart in mouth, he reached for his dagger and backed towards the rood screen, a rushing sound in his ears.

Behind him, Kirkpatrick's voice echoed from the nave. "Rob!" Swords scraped from scabbards and Robert sensed Red Comyn's followers and his facing off in the main part of the church.

"Two witnesses to your treachery plus the word of my spies?" Red Comyn grinned, pacing after Robert. "Add to that some servants to torture. You offered me your lands, Carrick? I think King Edward will give them to me anyway."

Robert whipped out his dagger and brought it down.

Red Comyn laughed. His scarred left hand pawed at Robert's wrist, caught it before the dagger could land. The mighty fingers ground into Robert's bones.

With his left hand, Robert reached for Red Comyn's belt dagger, yanked it free and drove it into the big man's side.

Red Comyn's grip loosened. He howled, bent double and rolled to the ground—

—and Sir Robert Comyn was on Robert, sword whirring down at his head.

Robert's training took over. He raised his right fist,

flat of the gored dagger along his forearm. The blow clanged into the blade, spattering Comyn's blood down his sleeve.

Sir Robert whipped his sword around for a second strike.

Blood splashed in the candlelight and he toppled.

Sir Alexander Seton grinned at Robert. "You owe me, Rob."

On the floor, Red Comyn groaned and rolled onto his side.

Robert shuddered. "Oh God, I don't think he's dead. We'd better get away from this place."

"Not dead?" said Kirkpatrick, striding up the choir, sword glinting in the candlelight. "I'll make sure." Using the sword like a shepherd beating at a snake, he struck Red Comyn on the side of the neck. There was a meaty crunch and the groaning stopped. Kirkpatrick turned to Robert. "Now, lord, you need to make sure of the rest of the Comyns, or the lives and lands of all your followers will be forfeit."

The wind rattled the east window and the eyes of the crucified Christ seemed to bore into Robert. He dropped Comyn's dagger. "Oh God."

"God Save the King, more like," said Kirkpatrick.

"What?" said Robert, mind whirling. Then he understood what Kirkpatrick meant. Fighting the Comyns meant fighting the English meant declaring himself King of Scots. He was the one who would have to put things right, but the stain of his great sin would make him a cursed Jonah for all those he led.

"Get me outside," he said. "I'm going to be sick."

June 1314

Sir Harry hurtled closer, pennon fluttering and whipping, his eyes white orbs behind the lip of his visor-sights, his great ground-churning destrier charging straight at Kipper.

And Robert sat still, axe resting on his right shoulder. The blood rushed in his ears, but it was now like sea crashing around a rock. He was immovable, fixed, and that fixity passed to the rough tough Highland pony that he had ridden through a dozen skirmishes and ambushes.

The lance point came for Robert's chest, the pennon brushed Kipper's head.

Robert rose in his stirrups, leaned to the left—his weight making Kipper sidestep—and lashed out with the axe, putting the whole force of his hips and shoulders into the strike.

The axehead sheared down into the vision slot of Sir Harry's helmet, sheared through the nose piece that separated the two eye holes.

Robert had a vision of his friend grinning, all white teeth and crinkle-rimmed eyes. The shock of the impact smacked Robert's palms. The axe shaft cracked, snapped.

Kipper reared, turned full circle and Robert glimpsed Sir Harry topple sideways out of his saddle, the axehead buried deep in his helm. He hit the ground with a thud that reverberated in Robert's chest.

Kipper turned again, then trotted past Sir Harry's destrier which now grazed placidly on the dry grass.

The Scottish spearmen roared, two thousand voices chanting as one, "Bruce! Bruce!"

Still clutching the stub of his axe, Robert took up the reins and brought Kipper down to a walk. His limbs began to quiver. Sweat broke out on his brow. He sagged under the weight of his mail.

Kirkpatrick rode out to greet him. He still carried the banner, but the Scots held their line under the tree.

The cheers died away and the men waited in expectant silence.

This was the moment for a speech grandfathers would repeat to grandsons. Robert groped for the right words, something short and memorable, but the fatigue pressed in on him.

"God's Teeth, Rob, what were you doing?" shouted Kirkpatrick as they neared each other, seemingly oblivious that everybody could now hear him.

The moment was passing. *Come on.* Robert held up the shattered stump of wood and heard himself blurt. "I broke my axe."

Laughter rippled down the line of spearmen, but Kirkpatrick was looking off east.

Robert followed his gaze. "Flanking force. Let's hope Moray can hold them off." Robert wheeled Kipper to face the main English force and tried not to see Sir Harry's corpse sprawled in the grass. Hereford's knights were now mostly across the burn and shaking themselves out into ranks. Any moment now and they would advance.

Robert brandished the stub of his weapon and bellowed, "Hold firm. God is on our side!"

As the men chanted his name, Robert rode to the centre of his line, slid out of the saddle and handed Kipper's reins to a servant. The tiredness drained away. "For the love of Saint Mary! Kirkpatrick find me another axe!"

Lances like a moving bed or reeds, the English knights moved forward, first at the walk, then the trot.

Kirkpatrick planted a battered looking Gallowglass axe in Robert's mailed hands. He hefted it, feeling the balance. "It will do."

"Smile, cousin," said Kirkpatrick.

The English chivalry swept uphill, a wave of iron and horseflesh washing over Sir Harry's body. The lances dipped. Robert raised his voice above the thunder of hooves. "I murdered a friend to atone for the murder of an enemy."

Kirkpatrick shrugged. "God's like that."

The first rank of Hereford's knights rumbled up to the edge of the trees and discovered the hedge of spear points. The great horses balked, wheeled, stamped, reared. More knights piled in behind them.

Kirkpatrick laughed. He gave Bruce a shove on the shoulder. "What are you waiting for?"

Bruce pushed forward through the rank of spears. "For God and the Lion!"

An English destrier reared up, hooves flailing at his face, then thudded back down ahead of him. A lance caught his shoulder, snagging the mail, but the rider was jabbing from a stationary mount.

Bruce struck the horse's head. The Gallowglass axe clove its skull to the teeth. He sidestepped the falling beast, caught the rider under the edge of his helmet, took off his head.

Now, redeemed or not, Robert's wrath was upon him and he waded through Hell dealing death equally to those who deserved it and those who did not. Howling like wolves, the Scots came on in his wake and he sensed rather than saw axe and spear wreak havoc amongst the milling knights.

IN ACTUAL HISTORY

It's all true! Sort of. All the episodes come from original chronicles, including the Lion banner at Stirling Castle. The Comyn murder is a bit of a mystery. Even pro-Bruce sources admit that—like Han Solo—Bruce struck first. However, nobody really knows why. Modern historians doubt the legend that Kirkpatrick finished the job, but the Kirkpatrick clan motto is, "I Mak Sikkar (*I make sure*)."

Bruce and Sir Henry de Bohun really could have been mates. Around the same age, they were neighbours growing up in Essex. De Bohun was neither a young gun nor a black hat and died doing his duty.

Riding a small horse, Bruce *did* take out de Bohun with perhaps the coolest axe blow in British history. Artists like to show a knightly battle axe, but a chronicle written by the father of a knight who was there shows something two handed. A gallowglass axe is equally plausible.

ABOUT M HAROLD PAGE

M Harold Page is an Edinburgh-based author and history geek. His idea of fun is teaching his friends authentic Medieval German Longsword, and then trying to hit them.

KING IVAR

By Anderson Scott

The Norsemen of the House of Ivaring arrived in Scotland with the most noble of intent: seeking to bring peace, order, and unity to a land troubled by barbaric unrest. Hold on there, the stories got mixed up a bit. To be correct, the House of Ivaring arrived in Scotland with the least noble of intent: seeking to kill a large number of Christians and take anything shiny in their posses-sion. They offered only one thing in return to the people of Scot-land from whom they were robbing: fire and steel. All right, two things then, but to be fair, they did give plenty of fire free of charge to all of the people of Scotland, regardless of wealth or social class. It was very generous of the Norse invaders. Eventually the Norse gave the Scots so much fire without any request for payment, that they were welcomed to stay by the few survivors, and a new realm was established under the Ivarings.

The first King Ivar ruled well, butchering people only when it amused him, rather than as a matter of course. The whole of Scotland was unified under his leadership, as the old kings were deposed and sacrificed to the pagan gods of the Norse. A kingdom was established that would last for generations, as the Norse be-gan to settle in their new homes, and settlers from Scandinavia arrived, displacing those who had had the audacity to call these lands home before they were conquered. The second King Ivar the people of Scotland do not talk about. It is in the dusk of the reign of the third King Ivar, in the final hours of his life, when Scotland was plagued with war and, well, plague, that our story takes place. Scotland was in a moment of darkness and needed a king to lead it, one with wit and aplomb, able to shoulder the woes of his people, and to help leave the dark and bring the land fully into the light of peace and prosperity once more.

***

"DAAAAAAAAAAAAAAMMMMMMMMMMMM MMMNNNNNNNNNIT!" shouted King Ivar III. "All we wanted was a daughter! Are these useless women capable of creating anything without a penis? I have been promising the King of Denmark a bride of my family for years, and have only been disappointed!" A powerful and large man, Ivar was shouting at his Council, gathered in the council room of the citadel of Ivar, capital of the county of Ivar, which was the seat of power in the Jarldom of Ivar, known to the locals as Albany. The family of the Ivarings were never truly noted for their originality of names, and over the course of Ivar III's reign over Scotland, eleven new Norse settlements on the island were founded, all named Ivar. The castle was of fairly standard construc-tion, with a stone wall and palisade protecting the inte-rior keep, storage, and barracks within. The gates were sealed tightly shut and the guards maintained a con-stant vigil, watching the numerous war camps sur-rounding the castle and the giant fires that illuminated them. Occasionally one of the inhabitants of the camps would get too close to the walls, and be rewarded for his efforts with a well-aimed arrow in the eye.

The council room itself was one of the largest in the castle and mainly filled with a single massive wood table and its attendant chairs, where in happier times more private conversations would be held about the fates of the kingdom. The king himself was adorned in the robes of his office, along with a flowing cape which he felt made him look regal, and most observers refrained from mentioning that capes are typically supposed to be worn down one's back, not their front. The discretion of those around the king was due widely to the vast respect they had for him as their ruler, but more directly, due to the large battleaxe he had a fondness for carrying around at all times. Physically he was a large person, towering over most of those around him, and was known as a fierce Viking on battlefields and throughout a number of charred villages in Europe. He had gone from victory to victory in his youth, and won more than his fair share of battles in his old age, and still enjoyed the occasional foray into France to steal gold and women.

"Do these creatures not realize that every bloody son they produce is another one with whom we will have to divide up part of our realm? Do they have no respect for the future of the people of Ivar?" he continued to shout. "Which concubine was it that gave us this false gift?" He shoved the crying baby he had been holding into the hands of his Steward, Dag Gautke, a small and nervous man, who frequently served as the most readily available physical and verbal punching bag to the erratic king. He was already the figure of a nervous and uneasy man, and the recent laws forbidding the wearing of pants in the royal presence did not improve matters in the drafty castle. Dag felt enormous relief that the king was not yet blaming any of the courtiers around him, and was quick to provide a new venue for the distribution of imminent wrath. "That would be the concubine you captured during the last raid into Ireland, your majesty, her name is—"

"We do not keep track of their names you insolent fool! Was it the redhead, the fat one, or the one that keeps praying to a blanket?" King Ivar interrupted. "The redhead, your majesty," replied Dag, starting to sweat. The other members of the Council began to back away, as the king began to stride meaningfully toward Dag and the crying infant in his hands. "You dare to refer to our beloved concubine by something as meaningless as her hair color you impertinent lackey! We do not tolerate such disrespect to our beloved..." here he paused as he seemed to be struggling to remember something "...woman. The charge for impertinence is death!" The king in one single motion brought about his axe and swung it around, cleanly separating the councilor's head from his body. To the rest of the council it seemed as though Dag's body stood on its own for a brief moment before collapsing to the floor.

"Someone clean the mess up and someone else tell us what the infernal crying noise we are hearing is? We know it is not a figment of our imagination."

Two men clad in the garbs of peasants entered the room, with a bucket of water and other cleaning supplies. Both men had spent far more time in the service of the king in their current roles than any of the councilors had. Feeling a sense of pity for the councilors, the two carefully avoided making any eye contact as one grabbed the body of Dag under both arms and dragged it out of the room, while carefully bracing the severed head within the upper clothing of the body. The other remained, carefully attempting to wash away the blood, and managing this while completely and intentionally failing to acknowledge the screaming newborn on the floor.

With Dag gone, this left only three members of the council in the room. The chancellor, the fifth member of the council, was down in the stables being fed ample amount of hay, and cared for by the livery staff. Those who remained served as the king's high goði, his marshal, and his master of spies. The goði, Gunnhilder, was the highest religious voice in the land, and was a frequent source of consultation for the king. She was also a woman, a fact somehow persistently missed by the king over the past two years, even though she could not and would not conceal that fact, frequently even bringing it directly to the king's attention. In one case, memorable for the whole court, she had even stripped down, displaying what the king had referred to as the feminine "fatal flaw" to all. The king had even failed to recognize that she had removed any clothing at all. In recent months she had given up on the effort, and proved a dedicated servant to the kingdom, helping and giving spiritual aid and wisdom to all who approached her.

The master of spies was a different sort of man altogether. As an example, he was actually a man. Formerly mayor of the town of Perth (now Ivar), Kenneth was a native Scot, and the only one to ever serve on the council. A long-time sufferer of the Great Pox, bouts of Camp Fever, and illnesses of all types, he had also been struck once on the head by king, who was learning how to use a mace. For the time being, he was the only one sitting, and occasionally dribbling or muttering. He was over seventy years of age, and completely bereft of hair, and never left the council hall, receiving his food and drink from an array of servants. King Ivar III frequently referred to him as "our most trusted adviser" and insisted that the spymaster never be allowed to leave the council chamber, where he had been for the past three years.

The marshal was the longest sitting member of the council, and easily the most ambitious and clever of the bunch. Anundur Yngling was the Jarl of Moray, and had managed to remain both in control of his title and stay alive while in service of the king for the past ten years. He had wisely taken to attending council sessions in full plate armor, forged by the most skilled blacksmiths in Norway. His armor was specially designed to have reinforced neck protection, with steel folded multiple times to prevent penetration by the sharpest blades. Technically the king had attempted to execute him personally no less than twenty times over Anundur's term of service, so despite the cost of the armor being enough to feed a village for the year, he felt it was well worth the price. Whenever another council member would be abruptly "retired" by the actions of the king, Anundur was the one who would step in and fulfill the duties of that member until a replacement could be found. Most credited him with being the one who truly kept the kingdom running and from falling into even worse chaos than it already encountered.

Angered by the continuing silence, the king once more demanded an answer. "By Odin, what is that infernal screeching?" Seeing neither of his fellow council members make a move, Jarl Anundur swept down and picked up the fallen infant from where it had been dropped at the time of Dag's demise. He responded to the king by stating, "It is your son, my lord, newly born."

"Oh," the king flatly responded. "Well, name it Ivar and give it to one of the nurses downstairs." Anundur handed the child off to the remaining peasant in the room, who had just finished his cleaning and quickly attempted to exit the room before he attracted any further attention. Unfortunately, the king spotted this motion and shouted, "Wait! Peasant!" Stunned, the peasant issued a silent prayer to his god, clutching the child in his hands and certain that the end had at last come, slowly turning to face the monarch. "Tell the guards outside to bring us the redhead whore and our woman-killing ax, we are not to tolerate another woman around here who keeps birthing males!" the king ordered. Nodding, the peasant rushed out the door, thankful for his life spared once again from the king's unfortunate and unpredictable whims.

"Now, how fare my beloved sons?" the king inquired of his council. With the birth of the latest child, the king now had seven sons, each of a different mother. Only two such mothers survived for the time being. One, the Queen Consort, continued her imprisonment in the dungeons where she had been for the past twenty years. She was widely considered to be one of the more fortunate mothers to the king's children. The projected lifespan of the other surviving mother, that of the latest son, seemed greatly shortened in the past few minutes.

"Björn, Fróði, and Karl are leading the army that currently marches to our aid, your majesty," Anundur responded. He chose not to elaborate on that topic, continuing with the status of the king's sons. "Sverker, Ivar, and Ivar are currently in various other castles across the kingdom under tutelage by those who you assigned them to. The most recent Ivar is currently on his way to the nursery downstairs." The sons of the king were fortunate to have skilled guardians and protectors after they left the castle of the king himself. Most proved to turn out to be functional human beings horrified by what their father was and what they could become, rarely returning to visit. The three adult sons were constantly jockeying for larger shares of inheritance and it was said that on the battlefield, they usually had as much to fear from each other as they would the enemy. The others were too young for this sort of intrigue, but were being developed as pawns in a myriad of plots and political games by the nobility of Scotland. Typically, the king ceased to care about his sons' fates once they left the king's castle, but occasionally, as now, Ivar III would ask about his largely forgotten progeny. Occasionally they impressed him, but that was as rare of an occasion as the appearance of the beast said to live in Loch Ness.

The pittance of statements offered by Anundur appeared to satiate the king fleeting interest in his sons' status. King Ivar sat down once more at the head of the council table and Anundur and Gunnhilder followed by taking their own assigned seats. Kenneth, of course, was already seated, strapped down in the assigned chair he had been kept in over the past few years. The king opened his mouth as though to speak, but no words came out, instead, the king stared blankly and straight ahead into the distance. Familiar with the king's occasional vacant moments, neither of the councilors spoke, choosing to remain silent and await further developments.

This continued for some time.

The state of affairs continued.

Despite his best efforts to be silent, Anundur coughed, and both he and Gunnhilder looked anxiously at the king to see if some offense had been registered. The king made no motion and the council once more sat in silence.

Silence proceeded to last a bit longer.

At last the quiet was broken as the king turned to the council and stated, "Well? Are you two quite insane? You've been sitting around not doing anything for who knows how long! We have much to discuss, and a kingdom that needs to be run, and protected from the evil doers who would see us cast down! Let us discuss the military situation first, Jarl Anundur, you have the floor, are there any military issues of note?"

"My lord, the peasants continue to lay siege to Ivar, and our last word from the army is that they are still returning from the most recent raids in England. They will arrive in a few weeks to break the siege and crush the rebels."

"What peasant rebellion? How dare they attack Ivar!" the king exclaimed and then paused for a moment. "Which Ivar?"

Sighing, Anundur replied, "This one sir, they're right outside the castle. We've been under siege for two months your majesty." The castle Ivar had indeed been besieged for some time by a peasant uprising in Scotland. The fires burning in the camps around the castle had kept a constant red glow upon the fortifications through the nights and the occasional shabbily assembled siege weapons would hurl flaming projectiles into the courtyard. Apparently, a number of peasants had tired of random purges and executions, not to mention oppressive rule by their Norse overlords who had assaulted the chapels and churches of the Scots and stolen everything not nailed down, and most of the stuff that was nailed down too. Led by a former soldier of the old Scottish kings who had been deposed by House Ivaring, the rebels sought to eventually take the castle and repay King Ivar for his attacks upon them. The castle was well provisioned and prepared for such a siege, but the army was away in England, and the situation seemed likely to continue until they could return. Every day the king had to be informed that a siege was in progress, and he was equally surprised with each new day's announcement of the same. The council simply awaited the conclusion of that particular rant which they had heard over fifty times now, once for every day the castle had been under siege.

As it always happened, eventually the words stopped coming out so fast and the spittle stopped flying. Calming down, the king inquired as to the defenses prepared for the castle and the forces within. A quick briefing established that the army inside the walls consisted of the majority of the levies that could be raised from the county to fight the uprising. The levies themselves were outnumbered three to one by the assembled rebel forces. Another castle garrison existed, but was prudently bound to the fortification itself, and was ill-equipped to fight a battle in the open. After informing the king of these facts once more, Anundur braced himself for the usual continued rant and belittling of those who had failed the kingdom by not being able to foresee the future. Instead, King Ivar's eyes seemed to focus and an odd calm settled over the room. Unsettled by the newfound calm and peace in their sovereign, Gunnhilder asked, "My king, are you all right?"

With a voice of cold steel, the king responded, "Yes. Call out the levies, and bring me my mount. Prepare to lower the gate for a sally. We will fight the peasant scum out in the open."

"My lord?" Anundur inquired, "We are outnumbered and lack any significant forces which could make up those numbers in quality."

A bit of the king's fervor returned as he shouted, "I will not cower here any longer, and it is time for me to demonstrate my invulnerability. The pitiful arrows and steel of man cannot defeat a god, and I am a god! Glory and steel await us out there, and I will not be found wanting in the eyes of the other gods of Midgard! I will go to my horse, and you will join me on the glorious field of battle that we will now face together!" He stormed out of the room, shouting at the guards on his way out, leaving Anundur and Gunnhilder remaining seated at the table behind him. As he left, the castle began making the noises of hundreds of armed warriors being roused to battle. Similar noises echoed from the distant siege camps of the rebel peasantry, as a harmony of clanking, clattering, and animal noises could be heard across the castle and surrounding area. For a time the three people gathered at the council table did nothing but listen to the slowly escalating sounds of the preparation for war. Kenneth eventually made a gurgling noise which could have possibly been a statement of some sort. Apparently taking this as a signal, Anundur stood up, adjusted his armor and sword and began walking toward the door.

Shocked, Gunnhilder cried, "You're not actually joining him out there are you?"

Anundur laughed and stated, "That was the plan, yes, he ordered me to join him on the glorious field of battle, I believe you were present for that particular statement."

"The king sick in the mind, we all know that, cursed by the gods with his madness. To join him now will end in only your death. Do not join him in that insanity. The gods will forgive you for not following a madman into a fight!" exclaimed Gunnhilder.

"The king is mad, that much is true. Some of the things he has done could be considered laughable or amusing to those of us who live in luxury, but there is nothing truly funny about what he has done as king. He suffers a madness that can seem contagious, bringing only decay and devastation to everything that surrounds him. His madness has spread from Thurso to Berwick, and it grows only worse as he ages. Still, I often wonder if he is the only completely sane person on this earth. He recognizes the inherent insanity of the world and embraces it, throwing himself into it completely, and enjoying the resulting chaos with glee. He has found amusement in the world, and he has the power to amuse himself more totally than anyone else. Through his power, he has found the game that runs the lives of men, and he plays it with every passing day, dictating the fates and futures of other mortals. For those within the kingdom, they are the pieces to his game, and they are totally under his control. The game of life and death is one that is usually only played by the gods, but King Ivar was able to find his way to a seat at that table. It seems that now, whether he realizes it or not, he has chosen to vacate that seat. I intend to make sure that the game ends for him as smoothly as possible in the coming fight."

"Are you saying what it sounds like you are saying? Will you really strike down the king in the heat of battle?" Gunnhilder asked.

Anundur gave a smile and said, "We've had fun over the years, and our own play has been fun enough, but it's time for me to take a larger role in the game of the king." As he walked out the door he said, "Most of the time the players play the game, but every once in a while, the game can play the players."

Anundur left and Kenneth gave a bit of a grunt apparently acknowledging what took place, though really it was anyone's guess what the hulk of a man was saying. Gunnhilder let out a laugh, because sometimes that was all you could really do. Well, maybe not all you could do. The windows in the council room were mostly small slits, capable of letting light in during the day but not much else. They were high enough above the rest of the citadel to see everything taking place within and most of the field directly outside of the castle too, and Gunnhilder went to the first one to witness the events to come. She had always had good eyes, and she, more than anyone, was able to view the final acts of the particular game played by the king.

The king had apparently refused to put on any armor and he marched out into the courtyard with his front-facing cloak flowing to each side. A group of people led the chancellor out of the stables, complete with a saddle and bridle prepared for mounting and armor for riding out to battle. The armor and other fittings had of course been initially designed for a horse, rather than a chancellor treated as a horse, and the poor man could barely keep up, being forced onto both arms and legs by the king throwing himself upon the saddle. Unfortunately, the chancellor, who had been imprisoned in the stable for a year or so now and fed only hay, was not in the best condition and he collapsed as the king's weight proved too much for him. This angered the king, and two peasant heads were soon rolling around in the dust until Jarl Anundur intervened, apparently softly talking to the King and encouraging him to instead use one of the actual horses.

There was a brief lull in activity as a new horse was brought forward and the king inspected the growing crowd of his assembled levy. Shouting was taking place and the soldiers, used to this nonsense, stood firm, and the king nodded his approval. As soon as the new horse was brought out and the king and the jarl mounted upon their respective rides, the impromptu army began to march towards the courtyard gate. Gunnhilder was not a military oriented person, but even she could see how disorganized the group was. Most appeared to have been woken from bed not long before, and others had never even seen combat in the open field. By contrast, the guards on the walls and gates appeared to be alert veterans, and a person could see the pity in their eyes as they watched the levy march out to what would soon become a battlefield. In this, Gunnhilder could see the hand of Anundur, as he attempted to prevent the worst losses in the upcoming chaos.

The disorganized force mustered itself outside of the castle walls, where before them the massive army of peasant rebels had gathered. Gunnhilder could see plainly that there were more than enough of the peasantry to overwhelm what could be called the king's "army"—a term fitting only as the result of misplaced generosity or optimism. However, whoever was leading the peasants clearly had military experience, and despite their poor equipment and clothing, the peasants were organized into fairly well defined units, and prepared for a battle; looking well rested and fed. The peasants did seem a bit surprised, though, that a fight was even being offered by the castle's defenders under these circumstances. Perhaps that would count for something when swords began clashing.

There was no distinct beginning to the battle. Gunnhilder witnessed King Ivar ride out in front of his men, charging the enemy lines. Jarl Anundur was not far behind him, remaining very close to his sovereign, while the rest of the army eventually figured out that it was time to attack. King Ivar stood out among the crowd of peasants like a towering giant, wielding his ax as though it weighed nothing and scything down seemingly dozens at a time. Encouraged by the apparent bravery of their king, a general fight began, but the tired soldiers of the king proved easy fodder for the peasant army, and most were killed by archers before they even reach the battle line. Gunnhilder let out an involuntary gasp when she saw Jarl Anundur dismounted by a peasant pikeman, and he disappeared into the mass of peasantry. The king continued to strike down those around him, until she thought she saw an armored hand reach out and pull him off his horse into the body of men. Gunnhilder fancied she could see a few flashes of metal for a few brief moments. The battle, if it could be called that, was beginning to come to an end, only minutes after it had begun. The few survivors of the king's army streamed back to the castle, only to find that the guards had orders to maintain the closure of the gates. The peasant army advanced, killing those before them, and eventually coming close enough to be fired upon by the guards of the walls. They fell back, and a status quo of a sort had been established. Gunnhilder watched as the rebels looted the fallen corpses of the soldiers who died in the fight, until she heard a humble cough calling for her attention behind her.

Three people stood behind her, two lightly armored soldiers, and a woman. She had red hair and was wearing only the barest robe, and not much else. She was clearly exhausted and recently weeping, but now she stood staring at Gunnhilder defiantly and refusing to budge. Both soldiers had light mail armor and one of them was carrying an ax, much like the one the king had taken out to the battle outside. This one was a little bit slimmer, and a little shorter, but just as sharp and deadly looking.

"We have brought the king's concubine here as he requested, my lady," said one of the guards. "Where is the king and what are his orders?"

Not sure if he was serious, Gunnhilder just stared at him. Kenneth let out a gurgle that could have been a chuckle from the table, and for a moment she wondered if he was more aware of what was going on than she had previously thought. As the surprised guards and red-haired woman watched her as though she had suddenly laid an egg, Gunnhilder laughed and laughed until eventually the laughter turned only to tears.

So ended the reign of King Ivar III "the Bewitched."

***

Word of the king's death eventually reached the army of the king's sons as it marched through the county of Ivar, only a few days away. The assembled nobility of the Norse lords of Scotland watched as Prince Björn became King Björn and awarded his brothers with their own new holdings and possessions in return for favor. They marched to avenge their father's death and the rebel army was quickly broken by the forces that had been assembled to fight the armies of the lords of England. For a brief time the new King Björn ruled justly and prosperity began to return to Scotland and the time of troubles came to a temporary end. Nothing lasts forever, and in time, the House of Ivaring fell and Scotland continued warily into the future, always convinced that the worst times were behind it.

Legends and prophecies in Scotland tell of King Ivar III. The bards spin a tale that his body was never found and that he never truly died in that final battle. They claim that one day the foes of Scotland will surround its people and lands and threaten it with utter destruction. In this time new plagues will ravage the earth, the trumpets of judgment will sound, and invaders will rampage through the streets, savaging the finest things that the Scots have to give to the world. In this time, the Scots will lift up prayers to their gods or god, and seek out aid and succor in the time of strife. In most of the world a besieged people in these circumstances will find little support from the gods. The legend states, however, that in Scotland's greatest time of need King Ivar III will return and most believe that he will only make things worse.

***

40

IN ACTUAL HISTORY

In the middle of the ninth century, an army of Vikings, known as the Great Heathen Army invaded Britain, taking large swathes of territories from the Anglo-Saxons who inhabited the region at the time. Scotland avoided the worst of the wrath of the Vikings and during this time some of the greatest kings of Scotland, or what was known as Alba at the time, reigned over the Scottish people. The men who led the Great Heathen Army were known to be the sons of the famed and possibly legendary Viking, Ragnar Lodbrok. In this story, I extract a story from a larger history that could have been, as though one of Lodbrok sons could have departed his brothers and led another force in conquest of the young Scottish kingdom that existed at the time. This story takes place in the end of the reign of a completely fictional man who could have followed as a king in a Scotland that had been languishing under Norse rule by the descendants of one of Ragnar's sons, known to history as Ivar the Boneless.

ABOUT ANDERSON SCOTT

I, Anderson Scott, reside in the United States of America in the state of Florida. I was cursed as a young child with a name and surname that by standards in the United States are backwards. Currently I work in law enforcement at a local-level agency performing analysis and data entry. I am married and have no children yet, but two cats who are persistent saboteurs of any attempts to write or play video games. In my free time I typically play a wide variety of video games, including Paradox Interactive selections, among a number of exploration-based games of a multitude of genres and types. When not playing video games, I enjoy board gaming and going out for the occasional camping or road trip throughout the country.

Anderson Scott is one of the winners of the *Crusader Kings II* Short Story Contest 2014.

THE KHAN, THE CALIPH AND THE KING

By James Erwin

The Caliph stared at the ground, his heart pounding in his chest, blood roaring ebb and flow inside his skull. He clenched his jaw, trying to make the thunder in his head louder, trying to drown out the screams. A bead of sweat crawled its way down his nose, more sweat curling and scratching under his moustache. He refused to raise a hand to his face and admit his discomfort. The bead of sweat pattered down on the dust in front of him. A flash of light knocked him to the ground and he felt a great dull pain begin to throb between his shoulders.

The horseman barked something in his gurgling, growling tongue, prodding the Caliph with a great ugly clout. One of the Armenians trotted up on a fine horse from the Caliph's stable, a smear of dried blood sprayed across its hindquarters.

"He says to look," grunted the Armenian, his voice thin and strained as he tried to speak in a manly register instead of his smooth eunuch's sigh. The Caliph made no sign of understanding. The Armenian descended and knocked the hat from the Caliph's head. He came in close, breathing hard. He smelled of pears and cloves. "He says," repeated the Armenian with a hard crisp sneer, "to look."

The Caliph raised his head slowly. His mind refused to make sense of the crumpled shapes before him, to define the darkness that stained the ground beneath them. He felt arms lifting him roughly and dumping him into a divan chair. Its perfumed cushions had been soiled, and the smell of that corruption mixed with the sour tang of the chair's laughing bearers. They heaved him up and carried him forward in a drunken lurch. He heard the children screaming, boys and girls both, and the women wailing. The bearers sang a song as they cruised the chair slowly past the field of horrors before the harem, shouting crude encouragements to their fellows at their red and terrible work.

The Caliph whimpered and clenched his fists and tried to fight the tears as they leapt from his eyes. He watched a life of sweet memories shredded and defiled and said nothing, did nothing. The chair wobbled forward on its terrible mission, to the river, which ran red and filmed with grease from the white bodies that tumbled in a grave and graceful parade to the sea.

There was smoke everywhere, a rising black haze that stirred the air and carried dark hints of brutalities in their thousands, small and gruesome souvenirs of all the sport his captors could not subject him to in person.

The Armenian trotted up beside him, his cheek trembling with the effort of maintaining his sneer. The

Caliph could not remember his name. That detail distracted him. He stared into the distance, watching a bird wheel patiently on a spiral of ashes. The Armenian peered closely into the divan. The Caliph looked back with the mild gaze of a turtle interrupted during a meal. The Armenian cursed and wheeled his horse around. Gouts of barbaric snarling spurted up around him as the Armenian urged something on the horsemen. Finally, they subsided into a sullen consensus and put the divan down.

The Caliph stepped out quietly, hands clasped behind his back, and stood before a small weed stretching from a dusty crack toward the sun. The Armenian padded up to him. Sniffing loudly to draw the attention of the bored horsemen, who were looking with yearning at a crime happening without them in the distance, the Armenian slapped the Caliph on his temple. The pain seemed to the Caliph to have a scent and color, a steel-blue thing that smelled like the scorched air curling away from a bolt of lightning.

"Enough of this play," snarled the Armenian. "The merciful and just Khan begged you to avoid this day and its bloody terror, judgment for which shall descend upon your unburied and unforgiven soul. It is time now for you to face your reckoning on Earth and in Heaven."

The Caliph said nothing and reacted not at all. The Armenian shouted something to the restless stinking barbarians to cover his unsatisfying response. They roared in unison, their gibberish chants resolving into a single word.

"HULAGU! HULAGU!"

***

The Caliph stood wearily before the great tent of the Khan. He looked numbly at the head of the Armenian, staring through dry and cloudy eyes at the ceiling from a wooden platter. Two boys appeared from behind a curtain and quietly whisked the platter and its gruesome cargo away.

"Your treatment was abominable. Of course, the wise and benevolent Khan has no intention of spilling your blood."

The Caliph shifted his gaze slowly to the courtier, whose smile seemed to hang on his dark and placid face instead of belonging to it.

"My children. My wives." The Caliph frowned and clenched his teeth to hear his own voice, parched and croaking. For all his solicitousness, the courtier made no motion to summon water or food.

"A conquest is a chaotic time," purred the courtier, "and warriors far from home are far from the memory of themselves and the sweet comforts of family. But I can tell you that any of your household with royal blood—which, of necessity, includes your cherished children—have not had a drop of their blood shed."

The Caliph frowned. "That is not to say they are unharmed."

The courtier bowed, his entire body trembling with feigned shame. "Highness, excuse anything I have said which may have caused you distress." A horn called and the courtier deepened his bow, almost sweeping his head on the ground. "We are now summoned before the Khan, my lord."

The Caliph nodded simply, his brow creased with thought. The courtier snapped his fingers. The horsemen paused ever so slightly before responding to his command and unbarring the way, and the Caliph noted with pleasure that the man blushed furiously, sweat breaking out on his neck and doubtless under his fine silk turban as well.

The courtier recovered. As he led the Caliph up the stairs of the platform upon the tent stood, he busied himself with his sleeves, preparing his grand gesture. By the time they reached the top, he was already fluidly lunging into a spectacular genuflection before the feet of Khan Hulagu, the brother of the Great Khan himself, the Conqueror of Persia, who had forced the Assassins to their knees and now stood lord over all lands east of Damascus, including Baghdad, the center of the Caliphate, one of the great cities of Islam and pearl of the East.

The courtier spoke these flatteries, and continued on in that vein for a very long time before he turned, shrugging as if to acknowledge a fly's buzz.

"And here, O Great Lord and Khan, is al-Musta'sim-Billah Abu-Ahmad Abdullah bin al-Mustansir-Billah, of the House of the Abbasids, Caliph."

Al-Musta'sim, the Caliph, looked steadily into the eyes of Hulagu Khan. The Khan was handsomer than he had expected. His limbs were short, but powerful, and the fine silken robe he wore did little to disguise the strength of the long torso it was draped over. He was surrounded by advisers and generals, some in the furs and leathers of nomad warlords, some in the black robes of Chinese officials, some in the robes and silks of Persia and Turkestan and the countless other nations that bent their knee to the Mongol. The Caliph bent his head slowly and slightly, the grave acknowledgement of a king in the house of another. Hulagu returned the gesture. His eyes moved over to the courtier.

"Dress your talk without so many flowers." The Khan returned his gaze to the Caliph. A small man had appeared at the Khan's side, translating into Arabic for the Caliph's benefit. The Caliph noted his presence reduced the courtier's usefulness to nothing. "They smell less fair than you believe."

The courtier bowed and scurried to the side, his brief part in the affairs of kings at an end.

"It is a pleasure to meet you at last," said the Khan. "I have unkind words of yours to repay."

The Caliph bowed his head. "I was assured your armies would scatter before the swords of Islam. I was told you were mere wild men. I lead my people in paying for my rashness. You are a greater marshal, and your men greater soldiers, than I could have believed."

Hulagu nodded. "Graciously said. I believe our audience can end on such a note." He raised a hand and horsemen moved forward to seize the Caliph's arms.

"Before you send me to my fate," said the Caliph over the talk which had already broken out, "I would ask one boon."

Hulagu's mouth twitched in a pale shadow of a smile. "Your fate and that of your realm are forfeit, and that I promised you long ago as payment if you raised his sword against me."

"I ask you to spare only a book. Let this city fall, as have so many others. Let my life end, as all lives must." The Caliph fell to his knees. "Spare only one book, out of all the treasures that spill through your hands."

Hulagu leaned forward, his curiosity kindled. His men murmured and he stilled them with a hand raised a half-inch.

"What book is this?"

***

The king is laughing. He strides the streets of his city like a lion upon the plain. His face is broad and dark, his muscles ripple under taut skin. A bronze sword smacks at his hip, oiled and gleaming. He drinks strong beer and caresses the back of a young girl. She trembles at his touch. He grins and encircles her waist between his calloused hands.

"Do not be afraid," says the king, and his voice is deep and loud. "No harm will become you. I am your king, your guardian. This will be a sweet night for you. You will eat at my table, drink my beer. Share my bed." The girl looks past him, to a sullen youth who will not meet her eyes or his king's. She tries to nod, and to smile.

The king follows her gaze. A note of something terrible enters his smile. He strides to the boy and claps him on the back. The youth staggers, and for a second a flash of anger brightens his clouded eyes. The king laughs to see it, and more to see it stifled again.

He bends down to look the boy in the eye. "Do you disagree with your king?"

The youth throws himself to the dust. "I do not, my lord!"

The king's smile is cold now. The market is quiet, save the cough of an infant and the curious murmur of chickens. "You lie to me. Good for you, to find such courage. But shame for you, for losing it again." The king curls a finger up and the boy, without seeming to look upward, shoots back to his feet. The ground beneath him is dark with urine. "I am your king. Through my divine blood, and that of my fathers—but also because I was born to lead. To fight." The king searches the youth's eyes. The youth will not face him. "Is there nothing in you to kindle?" asks the king almost gently. "Are you not a man?"

"I am a man," whispers the boy, "but you, mighty Gilgamesh, are a god. I will not defy you. I beg forgiveness. I beg."

"You beg." The king nods. "Laugh, instead, for I have favored you and your marriage." The king turns back to the girl. "At sunrise, this girl will be returned to your house, with rich presents and beer for your marriage feast."

"You will not take her." The king stops, whirling. He is smiling, thinking the boy has found some scrap of courage. His heart races; to wrestle a man, to spill just a bit of blood in a worthy, manly contest—too rare a delight, especially since it so flavored the joys of his table and his bed. But the boy is still trembling, not speaking. It is a stranger.

Gilgamesh grins. He slaps at his oiled chest, stretches his shoulders and holds his arms wide. "You are a guest in my city. You do not understand the custom."

"I understand it very well," said the stranger. Gilgamesh noted how like to himself in face and build the man was, dark-skinned and flat-nosed; yet his own spirit gazed back from the stranger's eyes. The stranger walked forward, unafraid, his feet planted carefully and surely. "You take what is not yours to take."

"Everything in this city is mine."

"Not my body," said the stranger, "nor my conscience are yours to command."

Gilgamesh roars with laughter. He unbuckles his sword and sets it aside. "Then I shall teach you to obey me."

"You are the one with a lesson to learn."

The two men grapple. They punch and kick, teeth bared. The stranger is a match for Gilgamesh in speed and strength. His soldiers cluster around, but none of them will act until Gilgamesh speaks. The men and women of the city back away but do not flee. The boy and girl clutch each other, neither one daring to seize the moment.

They wrestle. The sun climbs and sinks, and the ground shimmers with heat. They gasp and cough dust. They smear themselves with their own blood, and hiss and grunt. They fight, hurling each other against stone and dirt, into the darkness. By torchlight, the contest continues, until finally both men slump, unable to move, unable to do anything but lie on their backs, watching the stars wheel overhead.

Finally, Gilgamesh laughs. From some new well within himself, he finds the strength to stand and to laugh at himself. He holds out a hand.

"You are my equal. You are my brother." He embraces the stranger. "You speak honestly. You would be my heart. I would allow it. I ask only your name. Let me shout it to the gods."

"The gods sent me," says the stranger, "that I might balance and steer you rightly." He returns the king's embrace. "You are my brother, Gilgamesh. I am Enkidu."

***

Hulagu nodded. "A pretty tale."

The Caliph spread his hands. "And yet only one brief episode, among many. This tale of Gilgamesh is wondrous, and it speaks of the beginning of the world, of love and wisdom, through adventures that stir the soul."

"I do not know this legend."

"None do," said the Caliph. "A goatherd happened upon a tablet deep in ruins, and he happened to bring them to the one scholar in Baghdad who knew the ancient tongues. He learned them from stones deep in our library. Should that man die, all his knowledge of those ancient days would vanish with him." The Caliph frowned. "All except the tale of Gilgamesh, which I ordered copied into a single scroll."

"It tells the tale of this Gilgamesh and his brother Enkidu. Sent by the gods?"

"And tamed by the touch of a woman, who boldly shows him the soft joys and rewards of civilization, to throw aside the savagery of the forest for the tools of speech and law."

Hulagu pursed his lips. "You might have done better to start with that part of the tale." He stretched his legs and stood. The whisper and jingle of clothes and jewels and swords spread through the tent as all fell to their knees. "The tale amuses me. I shall give orders to spare the library for the night. My men have sport enough to last." Hulagu regarded the Caliph coldly. "Please enjoy the hospitality of my tent tonight."

The Caliph bowed. Two horsemen conducted him away, perhaps not quite as roughly as before. He spent the night tossing, unable to find solace in sleep or wine. The next day, he was escorted back to court. The Khan sat and heard petitions, sent messages, divided spoils, and all the while the Caliph heard the screams of his people and the distant tumbling of his city's mosques and homes.

Finally, as dusk fell and torches were lit, the Khan clapped his hands.

"Come then, mighty Caliph. Another tale."

***

Gilgamesh is older now, by a few years. He is surprised in the mornings by aches which have no cause, by white hairs which now appear in his curls. The streets of his city bustle as ever with life, and now that he has forsaken sport at the expense of the women, now that he no longer leaps to war and summons his men, his people do not fly at his approach. They do not fling themselves sobbing at his feet but bow low, with true gratitude and respect upon their faces. Nearly all: many still bear old wounds inwards and outwards, wounds he caused. For the first time, Gilgamesh understands those wounds.

Enkidu is dead.

He joined Gilgamesh in laughing at the great goddess Ishtar herself. A creature sent by the gods, he was recalled for his impudence, for the love he gave Gilgamesh at their expense. He died gasping, his skin slippery with burst sores, his eyes clouded with pain. It was Gilgamesh's fault. It was the fault of the gods.

"Accept this judgment," said the elders, and Gilgamesh's own mother. "Enkidu's sacrifice has washed away your guilt. Know the gods have forgiven you. Accept the path they have set you."

Gilgamesh shakes his head, in the quiet of his dark rooms. He cannot accept the judgment of the gods, for he has never offered himself to them for judgment. He asks questions of his priests, which they answer, trembling.

"I want to live forever," he says. "I want to be as a god. I defy them."

"They will strike you down," say the elders, "and if you do succeed, even then it will be their will done."

Gilgamesh shakes his head. "Tell me." They do.

Gilgamesh walks south, into the desert, into the mountains, into the marshes. He comes to the end of the world, to the great sea, and there he takes a boat to an island, which may be in this world and may not. He comes upon an old man, smiling at labor in his garden.

"You are Utnapishtim," says Gilgamesh. "The one the gods spared when they flooded the Earth."

The old man rocks back on his heels and smiles. "I am one of two. My wife is making dinner."

Gilgamesh sinks to his knees, holding out his hands. "You have been granted eternal life. Such wisdom. Such power. It must make you a rival of the gods themselves."

Utnapishtim makes a soft noise. It means neither yes nor no.

Gilgamesh leans in, his eyes glittering. "I would use this power against the gods. I would make a new world. It would be just. Fair. I could set everything to rights. Everything."

Utnapishtim purses his lips and stands. "Indeed. But first you must eat."

He invites Gilgamesh into a humble hut. His wife smiles. She is warm and gentle. Utnapishtim explains Gilgamesh's desire and she sighs, still smiling.

"If you would live forever," she says, "you must be a man of iron will."

"I am."

She stands. "I heard you talking and thought you might stay. I prepared a bed for you. But I think perhaps I have a different purpose for it."

She leads Gilgamesh to a room at the back of the hut. "Stay awake here for a week," she says. "Prove yourself worthy and I will tell my husband to grant you what you desire."

Gilgamesh stands for long, lonely hours. His eyes grow heavy, but he stands. His limbs tremble, his skin crawls. He hears his blood pounding in his ears. The light pains him, and the darkness calls to him. He bows his head, clenching his fists, digging in the nails until he bleeds. The ringing in his ears becomes voices calling to him, the women he wronged, the men he killed, the hissing fury of the goddess as she cursed his brother. The darkness envelops him, consumes him.

Gilgamesh awakes. Four loaves of bread stand by his bed, one still warm and rich in aroma. The others are old, one of them already turning green. He leaves the room. Utnapishtim and his wife sit calmly, smiling.

"We left a loaf," Utnapishtim says, "every day you slept."

Gilgamesh weeps. Warm hands close on his shoulders.

"Do not weep," the wise and ancient whisper. "You are a great man. The greatest of an age. But even the greatest man shall become dust. Our souls live on. Our words and deeds. Not our shells. Do not confuse your shell with your self. If you do, you can never fully live."

Gilgamesh rises and embraces the ancients, last witnesses of the world as the gods first made it. He sails back into the world. He walks footsore to the city of Uruk. The people rejoice at his return. He bends himself to his work, gravely and benignly. He rules with wisdom and love to match his early wildness. And when, in his time, he dies, his son sends his body wending on a funeral pyre to the gods.

They welcome Gilgamesh. They hand him rich robes, and unveil the truths of the world to him, and set him as judge over all men who pass into death. He laughs, for he has earned a reward beyond any imagining, and his brother sits by his side.

***

Hulagu leaned forward. The court fell silent at the look on his face.

"Do you teach me," he murmured to the Caliph, "how to rule?"

The Caliph shook his head. "I would not so presume. The tale teaches all of us what we would learn of it. And there is much I have not told."

Hulagu nodded. "So this gentle and wise tale is all you would beg me to spare."

The Caliph shrugged. "I expect nothing. I was mistaken. I was a fool. Ever so do fools with crowns end."

Hulagu laughed. "I am a Mongol. To remove crowns from fools is our greatest joy in this world." The court roared at his wit and fell quiet again just as quickly as Hulagu stood, and descended, to stand with the Caliph.

"It is unmeet," said Hulagu, "to shed royal blood upon the ground."

"I notice," whispered the Caliph, "this does not mean my life is spared."

"Indeed not." There was a trace of sadness in Hulagu's voice. "This book of yours. Lost how long?"

"Three thousand years."

"A long time. And but for the whims of fate, it might have remained buried a thousand more." Hulagu clapped the Caliph on the shoulder. "I shall spare this tale of Gilgamesh. Perhaps I shall have someone tell me the rest of this tale. Someone prettier than yourself, I imagine." Hulagu returned to his throne. "Time," he said.

The horsemen descended on the Caliph. He offered no resistance. He could smell the decay on the air. The Tigris ran red with blood, bodies bobbing gently as they tumbled to the sea. Already, riders whooped as they mounted and rode for the library.

A grand carpet was laid out, one from his own palace. Blood curled in dark spots along a corner. A horseman kicked the Caliph in the back of the knees, and he tumbled. Before he could cry out, the carpet was rolled around him. He could not breathe. The heat, the darkness, all was horror. A horse neighed as it was led over, three more behind it. An act of mercy, as he strangled.

The blows landed. Darkness shrouded the Caliph. He saw a bearded face awaiting him. He was going to his judgment.

***

IN ACTUAL HISTORY

In 1258, Hulagu Khan led a massive army to the Caliphate's capital of Baghdad. After a 12-day siege, the city fell. In the aftermath of the siege, the Mongols pillaged the great city and killed its inhabitants in a week-long massacre. Estimates of the dead range from 200,000 to over a million. The last Caliph, Al-Musta'sim, was captured. After witnessing the destruction of his capital and the slaughter of his subjects, he was (according to most accounts) rolled in a carpet and trampled to death by horses. This method of execution relieved those who believed spilling royal blood on the ground might curse those responsible.

The Epic of Gilgamesh, which the Caliph in my story tries to save, was not discovered in the ruins of Nineveh until the late 19th century. It's unlikely but possible enough ancient knowledge was stored in the Library of Baghdad to translate it – but as the story says, it's much less likely it could have saved the Caliph's life.

ABOUT JAMES ERWIN

James Erwin lives in Des Moines, Iowa. He's written for a number of websites and publications, including Slate.com, boingboing.com, Wired, and McSweeney's, and is the author of two historical encyclopaedias. His first novel, *Acadia*, will be published in late 2014. He has been a fan of Paradox games for over a decade, and cut his teeth as a fiction writer in the AAR forums.

THE DAUGHTERS OF
JOHN ANGLICUS

By Lee Battersby

It takes the cart a fortnight to travel from Salerno to Ostia. By the time she arrives, Trota feels as if she has aged a decade. None of her bones are where they belong, and the mute solemnity of the cart driver has long since driven her into an internal contemplation which only the strangeness of her destination rescues her. Despite the numbness, she gazes from side to side with open interest as the cart rumbles through the paved streets. Ostia is a seaside town. The sights and smells— even the sounds—are alien to her country senses. Gulls wheel in abandon through an overly-blue sky. The clothes that flap from lines strung between the two and three-story houses are a bright profusion of unknown colours. The language of the locals as they shout to each other like frenzied children is only vaguely familiar. Trota catches words here and there, but the accent is sharper, more nasal than she is used to. She may as well be trundling through a maelstrom of Frenchmen as her fellow Italians. After so long in her road clothes she feels drab, and stupid, and as dusty within as without. If she were a patient at her clinic, Trota would advise herself to rest in warm water and rub her ankles with salt. But there is work to be done, and she does not have time to rest. Such a summons as the one that set her on this road come rarely, if at all, and are not to be delayed. The cart slows as the narrow road opens out into a piazza, and she looks up in a paroxysm of anticipation.

It is beautiful, a cobbled circle surrounding a three-tiered fountain that splashes with a voice like singing children. For a moment Trota is lost in the splendour of the water, then in astonishment at the locals who trudge past it without a glance. Nonetheless, her sense of urgency overrides any further consideration. She nudges the driver, points across the plaza to the road rising towards the bishop's residence at the summit of the hill overlooking the bay. He doesn't even acknowledge her, simply clicks at the mule and spurs it on to a slightly quicker shamble. They rise away from the scene of rustic beauty, past houses that grow in stature and the ornateness of their façades, through roads that become avenues and, finally, broaden out into a square surrounded by buildings whose size dwarf anything she has seen since her arrival. A golden gate stands at one end: beyond it, rolling gardens border a gravel driveway that sends the cart up to doors wider than even those at the University where she makes her home. For a moment, Trota considers ordering the driver to turn around, to take her away from the towering frontage of white marble that looms over her, crushing her vision and self-image with its sheer presence. But the driver has already dismounted, and slung her satchel to the ground. Faced with his mute resistance, she has no option but to clamber down and watch the mule recede to the relative safety of the known world outside.

She is pulled from her reverie by a discreet cough behind her. She turns, startled, to see a tall, grey stick figure of a man staring down at her from the top step. His cleanliness makes her feel like a vagrant.

"Are you the woman?" The arrogance in his voice triggers a lifetime of insolence. Automatically she raises her chin, and returns his stare with haughtiness of her own.

"Are you the water boy?"

"I am Francesco, personal secretary to his Excellency, Hugo of Ostia."

"Oh." Trota grins. "No chance of you taking my bag, then?"

Francesco's gaze turns to ice. "Follow me." He swivels on his heel and strides along the front of the residency, not waiting to see whether she follows. Trota grabs up her satchel and dashes after him. He rounds the corner of the building and strides across a wide, perfectly smooth lawn at an angle. Trota catches up, and glances at him sidelong.

"So, what? I only deserve the tradesman's entrance?"

"You do not deserve the residency at all," he says without turning his head. "His Excellency does not wish to be troubled by your presence."

"What?" For a second, she is too stunned to keep up, and falls a step behind. Then anger overcomes her, and she dares to reach out and grab the man's wrist. "I beg your pardon? I come all the way here because he calls me, I abandon my studies—"

"You did not." He shrugs her off. "You were summoned by the Church, woman, not His Excellency. You would do well to keep your mouth shut and remember who you speak to."

The lawn ends at a high hedge a hundred yards from the building. Francesco leads her towards it in silence, and through a gap so cunningly hidden she cannot see it from twelve steps away. On the other side the hill rolls down a mile or so to a cliff. Orchards cover the hillside, and through them, a gravelled path winds down to a walled villa perched on the cliff edge.

"Down there," Francesco said, "Begone." Before she can reply he slips back through the hedge and is gone. Trota stares at the hidden villa. Suddenly, the days on the cart catch up with her bones. The thought of trudging all that way, with no real idea of why she has been summoned or what awaits her, seems too much to bear. Her knees want to give way, to draw her onto the rough ground. All she needs to do is lay her head against her bag, close her eyes, and never wake again. The hillside is silent. No birds cry in the salt air, no insects chitter in the surrounding leaves. She is alone in the world, a long way from comfort. For a moment she considers picking her satchel up and striding back through the hedge, marching through the gates and down into Ostia, turning her back on the summons and losing herself in the winding seaside alleyways for the price of a bed and a bowl of soup. Then she sighs, hefted the bag, and trudges the long mile to the villa.

Seen close, it is less humble than small in scale. The compact garden at its front is flawless, an exercise in geometric perfection that draws a nod of admiration from the weary traveller. Its low stone wall gleams white in the sun, and she can find not a single crack in its smooth, unbroken render. The gate swings easily on oiled hinges as she passes through. A man sits on a bench in the clean-swept portico. He rises at her approach, and reaches out to take her bag.

"You are the chirurgeon, Trota?" he asks in a soft, strangely-accented voice. Trota glances up at him. He appears to be in his fifties, past the full strength of his manhood. His skin is pale beneath a reddish beard, and beginning to sag across his bones. The hands clutching her satchel remember, rather than contain, a workman's strength. His eyes are red and wet, although they gaze at her with a keen measure. His hair is full, mottled red and grey, and swept back in a style she has not seen since her youth. Despite the gentleness he exudes, Trota is instantly wary.

"I am," she acknowledges. "And you are?"

"Call me Nicholas," he says, smiling to himself as much as her. Trota raises her eyebrows in surprise.

"Not an Italian name."

"No," he said. "I'm Roman by occupation, not by birth. Please..." He indicates a richly carved wooden door behind them. "Come inside. I'll show you to your room, and have a bath drawn. The journey must have tired you."

"Yes." She allows him to take her by the elbow and lead her inside. "I'm afraid so." She barely notices her surroundings as they wander through corridors towards a small but comfortably appointed room towards the rear of the building. He leaves her at the door with a promise to send for her when she has rested. Trota waits impatiently while silent women fill a copper bath with steaming water, then closes the door upon the world and lowers herself into it with a long sigh of pleasure. She lies with her eyes closed until the bath is too cold for comfort, then drags herself out and rummages in her bag for a clean shift to wear. Another soundless housemaid leads her to a small kitchen, and a simple meal of soup and bread. Trota demolishes three bowls before noticing Nicholas standing at the end of the table.

"Oh, I'm sorry." She wipes her mouth. "I didn't realise I was so hungry."

"No need to apologise," he replies. "The mushrooms are grown in the fields outside, and the sisters have more than they know what to do with." He gestures to a door at the other end of the room. "I think it's time to get to work."

Trota stands. "Yes, I've been wondering…why have I been called here? Do you know what this is about?"

"Follow me." He precedes her towards the far end of the complex, across a courtyard straining to contain a massed profusion of ferns and into a private sanctum. Trota has time to marvel at the richness of the furnishings as they step inside. Whoever this home belongs to, they have more status and power than perhaps even the Bishop himself. Finely woven tapestries adorn the walls. Busts and vases of immeasurable beauty sit in alcoves along the walkways. Thick, soft carpets embrace her feet as they walked. And everywhere, silent women in simple shifts of pure white move to and fro on innumerable, unknowable errands. Nicholas points her toward a pair of ornately carved doors at the end of a short corridor, and gestures for her to wait while he slips inside. A few moments later, he reappears.

"You may enter," he says, and when she makes to move past him, raises a hand. "I must warn you. You are about to meet a person of the greatest power and privilege. You will address her as 'Your Holiness', and show due deference."

Trota frowns. "Your Holiness? That's..."

"Remember." Nicholas opened the door and ushered her through before she could complete her thought.

Trota stumbles as she entered, and took a moment to process her surroundings. She is in a room more richly appointed than she has seen in her life, with fine draperies so expertly woven they glow in the light of a string of braziers, and rugs so thick they tickle her ankles as she shuffles towards the massive four poster bed that dominates the room. It stands flat-footed like some sort of mythological beast, piled high with so many heavy blankets that she can barely see the woman who lies amongst them. There is a moan, and movement on the far side. Something in the bed squirms. A blanket is wrenched to one side as a long, pale hand grips it and spasms.

"Go on," Nicholas mutters into her ear. "To her side, if you please."

Trota edges past the end of the bed. Once round to the other side she sees the woman more clearly. She is tall, taller perhaps than even Nicholas, and older than Trota expected, being perhaps in her mid-thirties. Long black hair is splayed across a bank of pillows, and her olive face is pale and drawn close in pain. A nightgown is bunched up above her knees and stretches tightly across the rounded bulk of her stomach. A white-shifted old woman dabs ineffectually at her forehead with a damp cloth. She scurries out of the way as Trota approaches, and shuffled from the room, crossing herself and murmuring respectful words as she

65

passed Nicholas. He waves her on her way, and directs Trota to sit on the vacant stool.

"This is your charge," he says. "She is close to birth, but for the last month there have been... problems. Increasingly so."

"Why..." She sits, takes the woman's long hand in her own, and gives it a soft squeeze. The woman turns pain-squinted eyes towards her. She clenches Trota's hand hard enough to hurt, and hisses as her gut spasms. "Why is there no doctor here?"

"She summoned you."

"I'm two weeks away!"

"You are the only chirurgeon to whom Her Holiness has granted admittance."

"You let her lie here for two weeks in this sort of pain. What the hell—?"

"Watch your mouth!" Nicholas's sudden rage rocks Trota back on her stool. "You are in the presence of holiness. You will *not* use those words."

"Holiness?" Trota stares at him in confusion. "What are...? Who are you?"

He points towards the woman on the bed. "You have been summoned to attend to her Holiness' welfare. The baby is due, and you will deliver it."

"Her Holiness?" The words are finally filtering through Trota's shock. She gazes at the pregnant woman, then to Nicholas. "Who... who is she?"

Nicholas watches the woman also. "Her Holiness Elizabetta IV. Pope of God's church."

"The..." Trota snatches her hand back as if stung. The woman on the bed whimpers at the loss of contact, then rolls over and grasps her stomach, uttering a guttural half-prayer that descends into a growl as her legs rise convulsively into the foetal position.

THE DAUGHTERS OF JOHN ANGLICUS – LEE BATTERSBY

"Heresy." Trota rises in one, abrupt movement, pushes past Nicholas before he can arrest her escape, and runs to the door before he is halfway out of his crouch. "Heresy." She pulls at the heavy wooden door, but it will not budge. "Let me out!" She bangs on it, pulls at it again, but it does not move. "Let me out!"

Then Nicholas is upon her, dragging her away from the door while she kicks and screams at him. The woman plays counterpoint, her squeals rising in discordant time to her struggles. Nicholas manhandles Trota back to the bed, and shoves her onto the stool once more. He kneels down before her and grabs her shoulders.

"Listen." He shakes her. "Listen!"

"No. No."

"I said listen!" Slowly, his entreaties and the woman's cries slow Trota's panic. She turns white-rimmed eyes upon him. He lets her go: slowly, warily, ready to pounce upon her at any moment. When he is assured that she will not bolt again, he leans back on his haunches.

"This is the Pope," he says. "The true Pope. Daughter of the line of John Anglicus—"

"That is a myth." The words are out of Trota's mouth before she realises. Nicholas raises his eyebrows in response.

"Who was raised to Pope and discovered to be a woman, and who was banished for her duplicity."

"Killed." Trota recalls the story. Whispered myths have persisted in the background of University life through hundreds of years, rising into the consciousness of every student who passes through the doors. She has been at Salerno for so long she has heard every variation, every minor detail, been disabused and educated by a generation of historians and priests. "Killed in the street and the baby destroyed."

"Banished," John replies. "To the diocese of Ostia and Velletri, to rule from behind the male Popes who could confirm the Church in the eyes of the people."

"Killed," she reiterates, her voice firmer, her eyes narrowing.

"Killed." Nicholas snorts. "Kill a Pope, you say? You educated woman. You think that could happen? That the Church could kill God's messenger? Do you really believe any man has the right to do that? No." He indicates Elizabetta. "The people could accept a woman Pope, especially one who had proven herself a wise and just shepherd. But once she submitted to the sin of carnality, she was forever more woman than Pontiff. She was brought here, to rule out of the public eye, and a replacement was installed to receive her directives and relay them to the populace as if they were his own. When she died, her daughter replaced her, and gave the Church a daughter in her turn, fathered by the only man who might be forgiven for assaulting her sanctity."

"You can't tell me—"

"Whether you believe it or not. And that is how it continued, through daughter and daughter, until Elizabetta was called to serve, and pass her instructions through her servant, and bear a child in turn. Until this moment, when her body labours to deliver and no result is forthcoming. And the Church is threatened."

"I..." Trota shakes her head. It is too much to absorb, too many lies to believe. Nicholas runs hands through his hair in frustration.

"Then see this," he says, and stands up. "A woman

is suffering. A woman who needs your help. For the sake of simple Christian charity, will you at least do that?"

Trota licks her lips. "Yes," she says at last. "Yes, I can do that."

"Finally." Nicholas smooths the hair away from Elizabetta's sweating face. "Your Holiness," he murmurs. "Your Holiness, I will return."

The woman grunts her assent, then lays back on the pillows and turns her face to Trota. Trota stands. Slowly, with great uncertainty, she bends over the woman's stomach.

"I..." She takes a deep breath, and her training asserts itself. "A bowl of water," she says to Nicholas. "Some rags, and the bag from my room. Quick as you can, please."

He nods, and leaves. Trota puts matters of belief aside, and sets out to ease her patient's pain.

***

It is dark outside when she knocks at the door again. It opens immediately. She shuffles through, to find Nicholas waiting on a bench outside. He rises, and she nods.

"I've made her comfortable," she says. "Any competent village doctor could have done the same." He makes to move past her, and she raises a hand. "She's sleeping. Let her get some rest. I'm going to do the same."

He nods, and lets her go. She trudges to her room, closes the door behind her and leans against it. When she is sure nobody is listening she loses her pretence of fatigue and races about the room, throwing off her linen and slipping her road clothes back on, and shoving equipment back into her satchel. She douses the lights when she is finished and waits by her window until she can see into the garden. She spies nobody patrolling the dark, no couriers or guards traversing the paths. Quietly she slips through the bedroom door, steals along corridors unnoticed until she finds a door leading out into the night, and unlatches it. Then she is outside, back bent as she dashes from shadow to shadow, through the gate and into the orchard, racing for the hedge at the top of the hill.

She is in sight of escape when soldiers step out of the darkness and bar her way. The pale, ascetic face of the Bishop's secretary appears behind them.

"Francesco!" Trota drops her satchel and holds her hands out to him. "Please. Let me pass, please."

"The woman," Francesco says to himself in surprise, then, "I have received no authorisation. This is utterly deplorable."

"Francesco, please." She waves towards the villa, invisible in the dark. "Down there," she says. "I must get to—"

"You shall not tramp through his Excellency's grounds at this time of night. I will not have...Your Holiness!" Francesco blanches, then drops to one knee. Trota spins around, her heart freezing at the thought of the heavily pregnant Elizabetta labouring up the steep incline in pursuit of her.

"Nicholas!"

"Quiet, woman." Francesco's hissed warning goes unheeded. The tall, white figure before them nods to the guards, and they instantly disperse.

"Thank you, Francesco," he says, and holds out his hand. Francesco kisses it.

"Your Holiness."

"Go back to bed."

"Your Holiness?"

"We will be fine, thank you."

"Of course, Your Holiness. Thank you, your Holiness." Francesco hurries through the hedge, leaving them alone. Nicholas glances down at her satchel.

"Disobeying a Papal summons?" he says quietly. "That is a serious matter, Trota."

Trota shakes her head. "That…" she begins. "She…" She points down the hill, doing her best not to shake, not to reveal her fear in front of this quiet, dangerous man. He smiles sadly.

"Yes," he says. "She is. But even if you do not believe, that is not the summons to which I referred."

"What? But you…" And then she stops. "You," she says. "You are…"

"I am Nicholas of Bedford, who is also called Breakspear. I am ordained Adrian IV. And I serve the Church and the woman you refuse to acknowledge as my master."

Trota's lips move, but no sound emerges. Then her legs give way, and she is kneeling before him, her hands clasped to her breast. "Forgive me," she begs. "Forgive me, your Holiness. I did not know. Please, please forgive me…"

"Get up." She does so, wiping clumsily at her knees as she rises. He reaches down and retrieves her satchel. "I am not so young as I was," he says as he hands it to her. "These nights play havoc on my joints." He turns, and begins to stroll down the hill. "I will visit Elizabetta in half an hour," he says over his shoulder. "You will attend me, please."

Trota watches him diminish in the dark. Then, slowly, she hefts her bag and follows him.

***

The woman on the bed turns in her sleep, searching for a comfort that is no longer there. Trota stands next to Nicholas and looks down at her.

"I am almost 55 years old," Nicholas says. "I was not expecting to be called upon to play a father's role. But Elizabetta's mother lived to her late eighties, and so she was raised to the Papacy at the same time I was. Such is the way of things." He turns from the dozing woman and regards Trota. "The Papacy has survived two hundred years of John Anglicus' dynasty. It is not for me to decide whether or not that is a good thing. It is God's will, not mine, nor my predecessors'. We are His instruments, as is the baby struggling for life inside Her Holiness' womb. It falls to you to preserve the succession."

"But..." Trota stares up into his wet eyes. "I can't..."

He sniffs. "You have performed a procedure. To bring forth a baby, alive. In the... caesarean manner."

"I..." She gazes at the sleeping woman. "Yes. Once."

"More than once."

"Twice. Seven times. Twice on a pig. To show students. But the mother..." She turns to him, her face bright with anxiety. "The mother dies. Every time. I've tried." Her hands rise towards him, beseeching. She lets them fall. "Every time."

"I know." His eyes are closed. Tears have escaped their corners, and moistened his cheeks. "I know what I am asking." He opens them, blinks away the moisture. "But the dynasty must go on. The Church must endure."

Elizabetta shifts in her sleep, moans softly.

"You're asking me to kill this woman."

"I am commanding you to save her child."

***

The room is empty. The Pope has departed, to lead the household in prayer within the villa's chapel. Trota watches as Elizabetta, the true Pope of the Catholic Church, struggles towards wakefulness and a day spent combatting the torment of her baby's enforced occupation. Her eyelids flutter open, and immediately close to slits. Her breathing is irregular and forced. Trota comes round the end of the bed to kneel at her head.

"He wants me to kill you," she says. "If you are who he says you are...he wants you to die."

Elizabetta raises her long hand. Trota takes it in both of hers, presses it to her face. "What can I do?" she says. "What am I supposed to do?"

"My daughter." Her voice is calm, despite the pain that causes her body to stiffen into lines of stress. "The Church must preserve the succession."

"But you..."

"I am nothing."

"You are the Pope!" She is surprised by her sudden vehemence. It is as if the touch of this woman's skin has removed all doubt, as if the smoothness of her words has washed away all resistance. She is in the presence of the most Holy, and she wants only that it should be preserved, forever and always.

"I am His servant. As are you. We are commanded to do this by a higher power than either of us can understand."

"You'll die."

"I'll rise."

73

"You'll die."

"The baby will live."

"But..." The thought hits her, and she feels so small and unworthy to even consider it that her face blooms red in shame: what about me? What happens to me, who takes a knife to the Pope and kills her? Perhaps Elizabetta understands. Perhaps she simply reads it in the intake of breath and the sudden widening of Trota's eyes.

"She who does God's will," she says softly, her fingers curling over Trota's own. "Is most beloved of God."

They sit together in silence, while the night drains away, and shadows emerge from the rising light. And in the morning, when the prayers of the household have been replaced by the muted sounds of anticipation, Trota unpacks her tools, and brings the newest daughter of John Anglicus into the light of day.

***

IN ACTUAL HISTORY

Little is known of Trota of Salerno, other than that she lived sometime in the mid-12th Century, and was a medical practitioner of some renown. Most of what we do know comes from one third of the medical text known as the "Trotula" and a handbook of practical medicine that was not rediscovered until the late 20th century. Much of the inspiration for this story derives from an account by Constantine the African of witnessing her perform a caesarean section for students at the University where she taught, a procedure rarely witnessed in Western Europe at the time. Pope Joan is a purely apocryphal, although well documented figure:

the female Pope who fooled the world until she gave birth in the streets of Rome, and was killed for it. A single text posits the possibility that she was banished rather than executed, and it is from this that I took the basis of the Order of the Daughters of John Anglicus, Joan's masculinised name. Two strong, powerful women usurping the masculine order of the day: I've been searching for a way to put them together in a story for years. Nicholas Breakspear was real, the only Englishman to ascend to the Papacy. The interweaving of two English Popes was too strong a lure to resist. The Bishop of Ostia and Velletri is historically one of the most powerful figures in the Catholic Church, and a permanent member of the cabinet that chooses the Pope, and old Ostia has been central to Italian—and before that, Rome—for centuries. If anyone had the power to successfully hide a heretical order of female Popes, it was him. All else is fantasy.

ABOUT LEE BATTERSBY

Lee Battersby is the multiple-award winning author of the novels *The Corpse-Rat King* and *The Marching Dead* (Angry Robot, 2012 & 2013) as well as the collection *Through Soft Air* (Prime Books, 2006). A children's novel, *Magit and Bugrat* is forthcoming from Walker Books in 2015. His work has been praised for its consistent attention to voice and narrative muscle, and has resulted in a number of awards including the Writers of the Future, Aurealis, Australia Shadows and Australia SF "Ditmar" gongs. He lives in Mandurah, Western Australia, with his wife, writer Lyn Battersby and an increasingly weird mob of kids. He is sadly obsessed with Lego, Nottingham Forest football club, dinosaurs and Daleks. He's been a stand-up comic, tennis coach, cartoonist, poet, and tax officer in previous times, and he currently works as Arts Officer for a local council, where he gets to play with artists all day.

TAKING PRIORITY

By Aaron Rosenberg

London, England, 1330

"Mother!" The young man shouted as he slammed through the doors and into the well-appointed antechamber. "Mother, where are you? I demand an explanation!" His headlong rush was arrested by a large figure suddenly stepping from the curtained alcove beyond and blocking his path.

"Your mother is resting," the tall, well-built man before him rumbled, his voice as cruel yet cultured as his appearance. "You should not disturb her."

"Stand aside, sir," the youth demanded hotly, though he found himself forced to backpedal a pace as the man loomed over him. "I require an explanation, and I will have one!"

"An explanation?" The gentleman's mouth twisted above his carefully oiled beard. "And what is it you wish explained, boy? Was it the riddle of why your mother might be tired so early in the day?"

The youth flushed at the barely concealed innuendo. Everyone knew what his mother and her paramour got up to at night, during the day, and at any hour in between. It was barely short of scandalous, and only their exalted positions protected them from reprisal or ridicule. He knew his mother's lover was attempting to distract him from his purpose here, however, and frowned, straightening and drawing in a deep breath before persevering.

"I have just been informed, sir, that my uncle, Edmund of Kent, has been arrested. I wish to know the meaning of this. At once!"

"Indeed?" The man before him stroked his well-groomed beard, most likely in a deliberate reminder that the boy was not yet old enough to grow one of his own. "You are correct. Edmund has been arrested. He is currently awaiting trial for treason."

"Treason?" The boy stared, incredulous. "Edmund? Don't be preposterous!"

Now the man's expression darkened, and his hands fell to his sides, where they bunched into imposing fists. "I assure you, this is no joke. Edmund conspired with others to overthrow the crown. He wished for, and worked toward, the return of his half-brother, your father—an act that, had he succeeded, surely would have doomed this kingdom and all within it."

"My father?" The boy could not have been more stunned. "My father is dead!"

"Of course, but there are those who claim otherwise." Innocent confusion was not an expression that came easily or well to the man, yet he attempted it now, wearing the pose like a poorly fitted mask that sat just askew enough to reveal the arrogance and contempt lurking beneath. "Fortunately, we were warned of Edmund's treachery and were able to apprehend him before he could enact the full extent of his plan."

Before him, the boy paced. "This is insane," he insisted. "Edmund would never betray me!" He stopped and glared at the man in front of him. "I demand to see him at once!"

"Demand?" Any false humility vanished at once, as the man's far more customary sneer returned. "I think not."

The boy refused to be so easily dissuaded, however. Not this time. "Remember to whom you speak, sir," he replied, his voice dropping to almost a whisper, soft and steady. "I am not some mere child, to be dismissed at your whim."

"Oh, I remember," the man assured him, one eyebrow raised. He executed a mocking bow. "Edward III, King of all England, Duke of Aquitaine." He straightened and grinned contemptuously down at the lad. "Your Royal Highness."

Faced with such open disrespect, Edward was stunned into inaction. At last he gathered himself enough to say, "Tell my mother to attend me when she awakens. I wish to speak with her about Edmund." Then he turned and, gathering what little dignity he could still muster, stalked from the room.

Roger Mortimer, first earl of March and unofficial co-regent of England, watched the royal youth go, not bothering to conceal his laughter.

***

"He is becoming difficult," Mortimer insisted to his lover later that day. The two of them were at Winchester, on their way to attend Edmund's trial and—Mortimer fully intended—sentencing. "Willful, obstinate, obstructionist."

"He is the king, dear," Isabella reminded him as they walked briskly toward the Parliamentary hall where Edmund waited under guard. "And he is seventeen. He is becoming a man, and men must test their boundaries and learn their strength."

"Well, he had best not try learning it against me," her lover warned grimly. Isabella sighed. She knew there was no love lost between her son and her paramour. Both were jealous of her attentions to the other, and eager to gain full control not only over her but over all England. She did her best to balance the pair, giving both as much of her time as she could manage, yet it was not easy. And especially not now, as Edward was becoming more confident and less willing to suffer under the yoke of her regency. In many ways, she mused, he was much like his father.

They had reached the end of the hall, and guards stationed there tugged open the heavy paneled doors for them so that the regents might enter. Parliament was already assembled and awaiting their pleasure, and in the middle of the floor, chained and guarded, stood Edmund.

The poor man looked wretched. Clad in only his shirt, bruised and battered and filthy, it was difficult to see in him the noble Earl of Kent, one of Edward II's most loyal supporters. Especially since, as soon as he caught sight of Isabella and Mortimer, Edmund threw himself to the ground, groveling like the meanest peasant.

"Mercy, royal sister!" Edmund cried out, his words ringing through the vaulted hall. "Mercy from you and my royal nephew, the king! Mercy, I beg you!"

"Mercy?" Mortimer sneered, leading Isabella to their place at the head of the hall. "I think not, traitor." He wasted no time in drawing from his doublet a folded parchment. "For are these not your own words?" He began to read from the document, which was a letter Edmund had sent to his dear brother, urging Edward to return from whatever sanctuary he had fled to and reclaim his kingdom. "The king, our blessed Edward III," Mortimer declared in ringing tones after finishing the recitation, "has confirmed that you are his deadly enemy and a traitor and also a common enemy to the realm; and that have been about many a day to make privily deliverance of Sir Edward, sometime King of England, your brother, who was put down out of his royalty by common assent of all the lords of England, and in impairing of our lord the king's estate, and also of his realm."

"I beg of the king my nephew, show mercy," Edmund called out again. "I was mistaken to believe my brother still alive, and knowing him to be dead I do hereby reaffirm my loyalty to his son, my own nephew, Edward III. I will gladly show my contrition! Set me on the path from here to London, a rope around my neck, and I will walk there though my feet be torn to shreds, crying out to all of my error and my loyalty. I beg this of him, by the royal blood we do share!"

Isabella might have been moved to pity by such a request, despite her hatred for this man who had stood with her abusive husband against her. Fortunately, her lover was made of sterner stuff. "Your plea is denied. The will of this court is that you shall lose both life and limb, and that your heirs shall be disinherited for evermore, save the grace of our lord the king." He gestured to the guards. "Take him to the scaffold at once, and let the executioner perform his duty."

Edmund continued to cry out, to beg and plead, as he was dragged from the room, out through the main doors and into the courtyard beyond. The members of Parliament looked stunned at such swift and brutal justice, and a few murmured here and there, but none dared gainsay Mortimer's decision.

Isabella would like to have fled back to the palace and their rooms immediately, but knew she could not be seen to be so timid. If those watching were to believe the sentence to be just, they must see her unfazed by it, and willing to linger until it had been carried out properly. Sadly, that took a good deal longer than expected. Indeed, a few hours later, an apologetic guard came to the chambers where she and Mortimer were impatiently waiting.

"Begging your pardon, Your Highness," the guard began, "but there is a problem with the execution." He wrung his mailed hands together. "The executioner has vanished."

"What?" Mortimer was out of his chair and across the room in an instant. "What do you mean, vanished?" he demanded. "Where is he?"

"We don't know, my lord," the guard replied. "He has not been seen since the sentence was passed."

"Well, someone else take up the axe, then," Mortimer insisted. "Just get it done." He turned away, as if the matter were settled.

But the guard remained. "Apologies, my lord," he stated, "but no guard would dare strike down one of royal blood." He was treated to a heated glare for that, but did not back down. "We are sworn to serve the royal family, my lord," he reiterated. "Not slay them."

Mortimer started to say something else, most likely

a colorful insult, but Isabella stopped him. "Are there any other prisoners here today?" she asked instead.

"Just one, Your Highness," the guard answered. "A lowly man, a dung collector, imprisoned for theft and other offences. He is due to be executed on the morrow."

"Tell him he will be pardoned in full if he will stand in for the executioner and do for our traitorous brother," Isabella instructed. The guard hesitated, and she frowned at him. "Now!" The guard fled.

"Clever," Mortimer admitted once they were alone again. "Such a man, base and depraved, would not flinch from any act that could save his own wretched hide."

"Indeed." Isabella gathered the folds of her gown as she rose. "Let us hope so. I long to be rid of this place, and done with this sad event." She frowned again as another thought struck her. "See to it that every member of Parliament who was present knows not to report these events back to my son. It would only make matters worse."

***

"...begged for your mercy, my liege," Henry of Lancaster was saying to a handful of others. Edward leaned forward, both horrified and fascinated by his cousin's recounting of the so-called trial. "But your mother and Mortimer would have none of it, and ordered that Edmund be executed immediately."

"No!" Edward whispered, barely able to speak. "And was he?"

"Indeed, sire, though not speedily or well," Henry recounted. "The executioner wisely refused to dispatch one of your own family without your word, and made himself scarce. In his place your mother and Mortimer appointed a convicted criminal, a dung collector, and granted him his freedom for killing your uncle."

"This is outrageous!" Edward slammed one hand down on the arm of his chair, hard enough to make the whole frame rattle. "I specifically instructed Mother to come speak to me about this matter, and instead she and her lover go behind my back and try and sentence and execute my uncle before I can intervene! And he begged for my mercy! Then, to be struck down by a commoner, and a criminal! That is no death for a Plantagenet!"

"Indeed, sire." Henry shifted awkwardly in his own chair, finally settling back with a sigh. Though a vigorous man in his youth, the earl of Lancaster was now past his prime and had been cursed with poor health recently, and with failing eyesight. Still, he was one of those who had been appointed to the Council of Regency when Edward's father had been forced to surrender his crown three years ago, and had always provided wise counsel ever since. The fact that the man had hurried back here from Winchester to inform Edward what had happened was only further proof of his loyalty.

"They have gone far enough," Edward mused, rising from his chair to pace the room. "Their profligate spending is like to ruin us all, their treaty with Scotland is shameful, and they are growing more vicious toward any who would dare defy them." There was no need for him to use names—all those present knew he was speaking about his mother and her lover.

"There is another matter, Your Majesty," one of the other men there, Edward's close companion William

Montagu, offered a trifle hesitantly. "Some say your lady mother...may be with child."

"What?" Edward pounded his fists against his side. "That is unacceptable!" To bear a child out of wedlock was bad enough, and especially for so prominent a lady as his mother, the dowager queen. But to do so when there were rumors that his father could still be alive, and to a man who had been his bitter rival and now all but ruled in his stead? Disastrous!

Plus, Edward realized, a child of Isabella and Mortimer could threaten his own position—even his life. Mortimer was a rapacious man, eager to claim every title, every bit of wealth for himself. If he had a child with Isabella, surely Mortimer would wish that child to possess the throne after him, rather than the son of his old enemy. And given how many people had accidents or simply disappeared when the earl was displeased with them, Edward knew he could easily vanish as well.

No, he would not allow that to happen. Not any of it.

"This has gone far enough," he declared. "I cannot and will not let them ravage our country any longer. I am seventeen now, a man grown, and have no need of a regent, most especially not ones so focused only upon their own greed and lust. I will sit the throne directly, and rule with my own two hands, not theirs."

"We are with you, my liege," another of the men, Richard Bury, declared. "But I would urge caution. Your mother can be a forceful woman, and Mortimer is like a wolf, quick to tear apart any in his path."

"We shall be careful," Edward agreed, "but we shall be decisive as well." He smiled, not a boyish grin but the careful smile of a man looking forward to a favorable outcome. "Mortimer shall learn that he is not the only one who can bite and tear."

***

"Curse him!" Mortimer shouted, hurling a goblet at the wall. It struck hard, the impact crumpling the soft gold, and wine exploded outward, droplets spraying about like a royal rain. "He has somehow turned the Pope against us!"

It was true. In recent weeks, every missive to the Pope had been returned unanswered. Yet somehow, when Edward sent messages to His Holiness, they received prompt replies and swift action. Mortimer was not sure how this had been accomplished, since his letters were all written in the name of the king and bearing his royal seal, yet he was sure it was true.

"Peace, my love," Isabella cautioned, resting one hand upon his shoulder. "We must remain calm. We will learn the truth behind this." She waved to the guard stationed at their door, and he nodded and rapped upon it with one hand. A second later the door was pulled open from the other side, and another guard stepped back to let a man enter.

"Your Highness," Montagu said as he paced toward them and then stopped to bow. "My lord." Isabella liked the young man, who was her son's closest companion, but she knew Mortimer did not care for him much, and that the feeling was mutual. "You requested me?"

"Indeed, my lord," Isabella replied, speaking quickly before Mortimer, still in a temper, could. "We wondered if you might be able to aid us with something. His Holiness does not appear to be answering my son the king's letters. You were recently in Avignon, were you not? Is His Holiness displeased with Edward?"

"Not at all, Your Highness," Montagu replied easily. "The Pope is very fond of His Majesty, I believe."

"And yet he does not reply when the king writes him," Mortimer interjected gruffly. "That hardly shows affection."

"On the contrary, my lord," the younger noble answered, with perhaps a touch of anger in his voice. "I have seen with mine own eyes several responses from His Holiness to His Majesty."

"And I have several that were not answered," Mortimer retorted. "Explain that!"

Montagu spread his hands wide. "I know only that the king seems satisfied with the replies he receives from the Pope," he said. "Perhaps these other letters did not come from him directly?"

"They did not," Mortimer confirmed, his anger making him drop all pretense. "They came from me, and my word has priority over the king's."

Isabella gasped at such a bald statement, and Montagu blanched, then set his jaw. "I see," was all he replied. "If you will excuse me, my lord. Your Highness." He bowed to each of them in turn, and then turned on his heel and strode back toward the door.

Glancing at her lover, Isabella saw at once the towering rage building within him. Mortimer opened his mouth, no doubt to order the guard to detain the young noble, but she quickly grabbed at his arm. "Let him go," she urged, too softly for Montagu or the guard to hear. "He is Edward's favorite, and my son will not stand to see him harmed."

Mortimer jerked his arm loose but said nothing, silently fuming as the guard once again banged on the door and it was soon opened, allowing Montagu to slip safely away.

"We must leave at once," Isabella said as soon as they were alone again. "Edward is beginning to come into his own, and will no longer tolerate our interference."

"Interference?" Mortimer all but shouted. "Who does he think he is?"

"He is the anointed king of all England," Isabella reminded him sharply. "And he is throwing off our rule for his own. Soon he will demand an accounting of all we have done in his name, and all we have claimed. It would be safer for us to be elsewhere when he makes such a request."

Mortimer glowered but stopped ranting and shouting. Instead he rubbed at his beard before nodding. "Nottingham," he said. "We will be safe there."

Isabella allowed herself a small, relieved smile. Nottingham Castle was a fortress, utterly unbreakable. With enough supplies they could last years there, and by then Edward's anger would have faded. He would be ready to forgive them.

Yes, Nottingham Castle was an excellent suggestion.

***

"They have fled to Nottingham!" Montagu announced as he burst into the king's private chambers, Bury and several others close behind him. "Your mother and her paramour are on the run!"

Edward glanced up from where he and Henry had been in quiet conversation. "On the run? Why? Has something happened?" He studied his friend's flushed face, his too-bright eyes, the sweat clinging to his brow. "Yes, something has, hasn't it? What?"

Everyone in the room listened as Montagu recounted his recent conversation with Mortimer. There were gasps and muttered curses when he reached the high point.

"Priority!" Edward de Bohun burst out, red with anger. "Who does this marcher think he is?"

"He thinks he is king," another, John Neville, answered softly. "And for the past three years he has been right in all but name." All their eyes swept to their true king, who sat stock still, hands white where they gripped the arms of his chair so tightly he might have meant to impress himself upon them.

"Indeed, John," Edward said finally, his voice equally soft but cold, his eyes sharp but not at his friend, "you are correct. Mortimer has been allowed to rule in my stead. But no more." He studied the lords around him, good and loyal men one and all. "Will, I want you to head to Nottingham straightaway. Take John, Robert, and Edward with you. Find a way in if you can, but if not settle in and wait. I will be along directly, with enough men to take the castle even if its gates remain barred." He rose to his feet, every inch the young king, and graced his friends and confidants with a regal smile. "Mortimer's hold over our realm ends this day."

The cheer that arose was almost deafening.

***

"You're sure of this?" Montagu asked the man. He glanced up at the steep cliff before him and the castle perched atop that—in the gathering gloom it seemed all of a piece, solid and impenetrable.

"Certain, my lord," Sir William Eland replied. "I've roamed this castle and these lands a full two score years, first as a boy, then as a guard, and these last four years as sheriff. No one knows them half so well as I, and I can assure you I speak truth."

"Very well." Montagu nodded. "Show us."

The sheriff led the group of men, twenty-three in all, around one side of the rocks. They moved as quietly as they could, hands clenching scabbards to keep their swords from rattling, and trusted the twilight shadows and the wind in the trees beyond to mask their presence. At last they stopped along a spot that seemed no different from the rest. But the sheriff grinned and reached out to press against a particular spot along the rough stone—and with a groan and a creak that sounded thunderous up close a portion of the cliff wall slid away.

"There you are, my lord," the sheriff announced, though quietly, and executed a short, well-pleased bow. "This tunnel leads up to the inner ward, past the fortifications. Your mother and her...friend are quartered near there, in the tower separating the ward from the bailey. The quickest route is straight across the ward, but if it's surprise you're wanting I'd advise you to angle back toward the outer walls instead—once you're within them you'll be out of sight to any guards stationed along the fortifications, and you can make your way around to the tower and up its stairs to the chambers at its top."

"We are in your debt, Sir Eland," Montagu told the man, shaking his hand heartily as a few of the others began preparing torches to be lit as soon as they were within the passage. "As is the king."

"His humble servant, and yours, sir," Eland replied. "We all rejoice that he will be sitting his throne soon, and we'll have no more of these pretenders."

With that, the sheriff left them, to return to his own

home in case anyone might notice his absence. Montagu and the others turned their focus to the narrow journey before them, and made their way, one by one, inside and then along the inclined passage, toward the castle above and its unsuspecting occupants.

***

"He did not steer us wrong," Edward de Bohun whispered after he'd returned to the tunnel—he had been in the lead, and had gone on ahead once they'd seen the end before them, to scout the lay of the land. "It seems to let you in a garden of some sort—I suspect there are other holes nearby, given the rock around us, and they are left alone as much as possible. I could see the outer walls behind the hole, and the tower up ahead."

Montagu nodded. "Very good. Now, once we're up, Ed, you and your men make for the main gate. Edward will be arriving shortly with his troops, and we want the way to be open for them. The rest of you will come with me—with any luck we'll beard Mortimer in his den and have him on his knees by the time the king sets foot inside." He frowned. "We'll need to be quick about it, as there's no telling how loud our exit may be, nor how many of the guards will notice. We'll have to assume they are all Mortimer's men, and will not yield even in the king's name." There were murmurs of agreement, and they all put out their torches, leaving them scattered and smoking there in the tunnel, and loosened their swords and daggers.

The men leaped out speedily as they could and sprinted across the gardens to the nearest door in the castle's thick outer walls, not a hundred paces away. If any guard noticed, they did not hear any outcry, and once they were all safely out of view they waited a moment but did not hear shouts or the pounding of rushing feet. They had made it safely into the castle.

It was late at night, and though there were undoubtedly guards stationed up above the corridors down here were empty and dark as the men hurried along, letting the few windows provide light rather than risking more torches. The walls curved around, following the natural shape of the cliffs below, and then at last branched off to the side. This was the juncture between ward and bailey.

"Good luck," Montagu told de Bohun, clasping his friend by the hand.

"And to you," the other noble replied before setting off, the handful of men he'd brought along right behind him. Montagu and the remaining lords did not waste time watching them go, but quickly continued their own trek, following the wall around until it came to the central tower.

There, at last, they encountered guards, though there were only two and the men seemed half-asleep from the monotony and the late hour. By the time they had noticed the intruders and thought to shout for help, Robert Ufford and John Neville had swords at their throats.

"Speak a word, and your life ends," Neville advised. "Go peaceably and you may survive this night."

The sentries nodded, white-faced, and allowed their weapons to be taken without a struggle. They were tied and gagged, and then the nobles started up the winding tower stairs. They could already hear murmuring from the top.

They had almost reached the next to highest landing

when footsteps sounded behind them. Fearing an attack from the rear, Montagu and the others turned quickly, but sagged with relief when the approaching torches revealed none other than their king himself.

"My liege!" Montagu called out softly as Edward reached them. "Your arrival is timely indeed—we are about to face the serpent in its very lair!"

"We spurred the horses to a froth," Edward admitted, grinning and sweaty. "I was loathe to miss this encounter, which I have been dreaming of for many a day."

"Then lead on, sire," Neville suggested. "And know that we are ever at your side, and ready to aid you."

With the king at the fore, they took the final stairs, prepared to confront not on the sentries they knew would be waiting there but the man and woman sheltered beyond them.

***

"Something must be done," Mortimer insisted yet again, rising to his feet and pacing restlessly. "We cannot allow him to undermine our authority!"

Isabella watched him silently, as did the men gathered at the table. There was little to say—it would do no good reminding him yet again that the authority was Edward's, not theirs.

A commotion at the door prevented anyone from responding. There were shouts, and the sound of ringing blades. Then the door was flung open and a dozen or so men stormed in, weapons drawn. And the first of them, his great broadsword naked and eager in his hands, was Edward himself.

"What is this? Treachery!" Mortimer roared, yanking his own sword free and charging the newcomers. But Edward was done cowering before this man. He met the attack full-on, blocking Mortimer's blade easily with his own, and then struck back, a deadly swipe that nearly beheaded his mother's lover then and there. Before Mortimer could think to retaliate there were two more swords at his throat, as Montagu and Neville flanked him. Seeing he could not win, Mortimer let his weapon fall clattering to the ground and stood motionless, hands half raised, though his glare did not falter.

Isabella had stayed very still during the brief conflict, lest a stray blow strike her down. Now that it was over, however, the council members and Mortimer disarmed and restrained, she rose carefully from her chair. "Fair son," she begged, turning to Edward and throwing herself at his feet, "have pity on gentle Mortimer!"

"Gentle?" Edward stared down at her, the scorn clear on his face. "I shall show him as much pity as he gave mine uncle, mother. Is that not fair and just?" He motioned for the men to escort Mortimer out before returning his gaze to Isabella. "The question then becomes, what shall become of you?"

Isabella stood slowly, doing her best to hide her growing shock and fear. "I am your mother, Edward," she reminded him, striving to keep her voice soft and gentle. "I gave birth to you, nurtured you, raised you, protected you."

"Yes, mother," the young king agreed easily enough, though his tone was grim. "But you also used me, manipulated me, and attempted to control me. Not to mention what you have done to my kingdom in my name." He shook his head.

"Ah yes. Your name." Isabella sighed and forced

herself to remain calm as she played her last gambit. "The same name as your father, and his father before him. The name that denotes your royal bloodline, and your right to rule." She stepped closer to her son and lowered her voice so that only he would hear. "It would be a shame for that name to be called into question."

Edward glared at her. "What are you insinuating, Mother?"

She smiled slowly. "Only that certain documents in my possession—or, rather, in the possession of those I trust—could cast doubt upon certain matters of inheritance. And parentage." She patted him on the cheek. "But there's no reason for those to ever be spoken of again, is there? As long as I live, they shall remain hidden, less than a rumor."

Edward considered her carefully. His mother was a clever woman, he knew—far more so than Mortimer, who for all his charm and cunning was too apt to rage and impulse. It would be just like Isabella to have arranged some surety of her safety, something that could ruin him if it were revealed. Were her hinted claims true? He had no way of knowing. But even if they were not, the very question could undermine his nascent rule. He could not take that risk.

"You shall be confined to Berkhamsted Castle," he declared finally. "And shall live there to the end of your days, in comfort but restricted to that castle and its grounds. And that will be the extent of my mercy. Are we quite clear, Mother?"

She curtsied. "Perfectly, my dear." Her smile was warm even if her gaze was cold as she added, "My liege."

Edward nodded and turned from her, back to his men. "Bring Mortimer back to London. He will be dealt with there." At last the young king allowed himself a wintery smile of his own. "Then we shall see who takes priority."

With that, they began the process of returning home. The king was now firmly in control of the castle, the region, and the country, at long last.

***

IN ACTUAL HISTORY

Edward II was king of England from 1307–1327 but was a poor king and widely disliked. His blatant favoritism of the Despenser lords led to a series of battles within the kingdom and cost Edward much of his remaining support. In 1327 his government collapsed and he was deposed. Technically Edward surrendered the crown to his fourteen-year-old son Edward III, but in reality the power was held by Edward II's wife Isabella of France and her lover Roger Mortimer. Isabella and Mortimer proved just as bad for the country as Edward II had been, and the people suffered greatly under their greedy, lustful rule. When Edward III was seventeen he finally decided he had had enough, and led a coup against his mother and her lover. Edward III's popular, successful reign lasted until his death in 1377, making him one of the longest-reigning British monarchs in history.

ABOUT AARON ROSENBERG

Aaron Rosenberg is an award-winning, bestselling novelist, children's book author, and game designer. His novels include the best-selling *DuckBob* series (consisting of *No Small Bills, Too Small for Tall,* and *Three Small*

Coinkydinks), the *Dread Remora* space-opera series and, with David Niall Wilson, the *O.C.L.T.* occult thriller series. His tie-in work contains novels for *Star Trek*, *Warhammer*, *WarCraft*, and *Eureka*. He has written children's books, including the original series *Pete and Penny's Pizza Puzzles*, the award-winning *Bandslam: The Junior Novel*, and the #1 best-selling *42: The Jackie Robinson Story*. Aaron has also written educational books on a variety of topics and over seventy roleplaying games, such as the original games *Asylum*, *Spookshow*, and *Chosen*, work for White Wolf, Wizards of the Coast, Fantasy Flight, Pinnacle, and many others, and both the Origins Award-winning *Gamemastering Secrets* and the Gold ENnie-winning *Lure of the Lich Lord*. He is the co-creator of the *ReDeus* series, and one of the founders of Crazy 8 Press. Aaron lives in New York with his family.

DAUGHTER OF THE DESERT

By Steven Savile

The bazaar spread out in front of her, so much excess, such temptation, everything imaginable for sale to buyers of discerning tastes. It was so different to the world she'd grown up with. But this was Constantinople. There was nowhere in the world like it. Even the air was different, the tang of the seas, the clash of cultures and the heady scents of the Orient all come together to mix with the sweat of humanity and the desperation of war. There were more familiar scents, too, spices; ginger, cardamom, nutmeg and paprika.

It seemed as though anything could be possible here. She wasn't used to that. Her world, right up until the death of her mother, had been a simple one amid the holy walls of the Sanctuary, sharing her thoughts with God.

The displays in the tented bazaar were seductive and inviting; the sight of capsicums and garlic every bit as alluring as the odors carried by the light breeze blowing through the narrow street. Trade was the lifeblood of the bazaar. Buyers and sellers haggled over the price of everything, but everyone in the bazaar was aware of the true value of the commodities down to the smallest grain. They had made a game of it.

It was a troubled time in the city. Constantinople was being used by soldiers from Europe to replenish their ships and take on supplies before traveling on to Jerusalem. Everyone in the bazaar eyed the soldiers with suspicion and distrust. This might not be Constantinople's war, but those traders were Muslim and knew that they should support their brothers in Jihad, but to do so would bring about swift and brutal retribution. Quite simply, they are not prepared to die for what should be.

Daunted by the press of humanity on all sides, drunk on the unfamiliar smells of spices and exotic food, Pashmira forced a way through the press of bodies. She felt hands on her, and felt their eyes on her, each and every leering face weighing her up like one more piece of meat to be bought or sold. It wasn't only food and spices for sale in the bazaar; young boys ran backwards and forwards with glasses of *Cayi* for the vendors of carpets and copper wares; the sweetmeat sellers wandered the pitches, hoping to inspire hunger pangs in the stomachs of the traders; and the peddlers of potions, unctions and cure-alls promised miracles. The tent city was a hive of activity.

And it was working its magic on her.

Hunger gnawed at Pashmira's belly.

She couldn't remember the last time it had felt full. Days ago. Weeks. The journey had been hard. But she was here now. This was her new life. For better or for worse, which made it sound like a wedding vow, which it was, of sorts, she was bonded to a new life.

Temptation was hard to resist. While thin men with

sun-withered faces gathered around the stalls, she snuck in behind them, and with hands driven by hunger, snatched a handful of dried dates from a bowl, stuffing them into her mouth before anyone could stop her. She chewed and chewed, the fruit tearing in her mouth, the little juice they had left spilling onto her tongue. She closed her eyes, savoring the taste.

But shouting broke that moment of sweet peace.

She opened her eyes to see three approaching figures; two crusaders in chain mail, a priest walking between them. They cut imposing figures as they pushed their way through the crowd. One of the knights shoved a woman aside with a gauntleted fist. She stumbled into a stall, and trying to stop herself from falling, toppled an earthenware pot, which shattered on the hard-packed dirt. A whimper escaped the woman's lips in place of a barely bitten-back curse. The crusaders ignored her. They were looking for someone and the crowd refused to make it easy for them. Again, this wasn't their fight. If they wanted freedom to trade, to barter and haggle and live their lives in peace there was always going to be a cost, and if that cost was someone the crusaders wanted, then so be it.

For one heart-stopping moment Pashmira was sure they were looking for her.

But then a scruffy looking monk with fetishes hanging from his rope belt stepped out into full view of the armored men. He glanced around frantically, looking for an avenue of escape, then dashed between two of the stalls.

"*Allez*," the priest cried, then the two knights charged through the gap that was too narrow for them, up-ending a table to the cacophony of copper pans clattering to the ground. The priest walked behind them. The crusaders pushed their way between the stalls, agitating everyone in the bazaar with their blatant disregard for anyone and anything that stood in their way.

Pashmira realized a fraction too slowly she was standing between the knights and their quarry.

She tried to back away, instinctively reaching up to wipe at the trickle of juice on her chin.

The priest stared at Pashmira as he reached her. It felt like he was judging her as his nostrils flared and widow's peak furrowed, before he pushed her out of his way and moved on.

Pashmira watched in horror as the crusaders caught up with the monk. One grabbed a tangle of hair from his ragged tonsure and hauled him back as the other slammed a gauntleted fist into the small of his holy man's back. He cried out for mercy even as another blow drove him to his knees, then a third clubbing fist took him in the side of the head and he went down.

Pashmira moved instinctively to help, a single step forward while everyone else shrank back. It didn't go unnoticed by the priest who raised a hand to stop her as though casting out a demon, "This is none of your business, girl," the hatred in his gaze was chilling.

"He's right," a man beside her whispered, laying a hand on her arm. "Not your fight, girl, be smart, stay out of it."

"But—"

"No buts, trust me. This is my city. I know what happens now. You don't want to be part of it."

He was right.

The beating was cruel.

The monk, whatever his crime, didn't stand a chance.

***

The man's name was Ketus Rinn, a merchant who dabbled in the sale of anything and everything when the price was right.

What he wasn't was her friend.

Rinn could be charming when he needed to be, ruthless when occasion called for it, and slippery as a snake when backed into a corner. For all that, his thought processes were simple. He had seen the girl, uncommonly beautiful even for a city that prided itself on being vain. He had known at that moment he needed her. It wasn't want, want implied choice. He needed to possess her. To own her, body and soul, but not out of any sexual desire. It was pure business; he knew he'd turn a decent profit on what was obviously an enchanting and dangerous creature.

"Are you hungry?" He asked, offering what he knew was a reassuring smile. He knew she was. He'd seen her steal a handful of dates. Someone who had a full belly didn't risk the wrath of the knights for a few bits of dried fruit.

"Starving," she admitted.

"Excellent. Well, not excellent for you, obviously, but I know just the place, the cook is a close friend, and she can work wonders with even the most basic ingredients. You have somewhere to stay?"

The girl shook her head.

"Ah, well, we need to sort you out with a roof as well, or the soldiers will arrest you for vagrancy, but first things first, let's go eat."

She followed him, two steps behind.

He had to glance back over his shoulder more than

once to make sure she was still there. Had she been more familiar with the city she would have known where he was leading her—to a house on a street known locally as the Avenue of Princesses because of the nature of the entertainment on offer.

He knocked on the door, three times, and smiled at the Nubian beauty who opened the door. She didn't seem to have aged an hour since the last time he'd seen her; a gift from her blacker than black skin, flawless and eternal.

"Noe Covi, as I live and breathe, damn but it's good to see you, woman."

"I'm not entirely sure I can say the same thing," the madam said, but her smile gave her away.

"Ah, you wound me, Noe. You *wound* me."

The woman looked at the girl he'd brought with him.

"You come bearing gifts?"

"My young friend here is starving, so I thought we might try some of Neta's cooking. Then, after we've eaten, perhaps you and I could discuss a few things? In private?"

"Of course, come in, come in, my house is your house. Come through to the comfort lounge, I'll have Neta rustle up something special for you."

"You're most kind," Ketus Rinn said, leading the girl by the arm through the hallway to a room filled to overflowing with silks and cushions and the sweet foggy air of narcotics.

He breathed it in deeply then sank back into the bank of cushions, accepting a pipe from one of the girls.

"I never asked you what your name is, girl? How terribly rude of me."

"Pashmira."

"Ah, the pleasure is all mine, dear lady." He held out his hand for her to take. It was all flattery, flowery words meant to impress the wide-eyed newcomer who was so obviously out of her depth in a den of inutility like Noe Covi's house. Noe was one of Constantinople's more influential madams, her house offering the entertainment of choice for some of the richest and most powerful men in the Byzantine Empire.

The food came, and it was every bit as good as he'd promised.

He regaled Pashmira with tales of the city while they ate, spinning out elaborate histories of the rise and fall and rise of the great city of Seven Hills and her architectural masterpieces, the church of Magna Ecclesia, the sacred palace of the emperors, the hippodrome, and the Golden Gate, lining the arcaded avenues and squares, promising to show her each one, even as he explained how so many artistic and literary treasures had been lost when the city was sacked. He made a face. He knew it was bad form to dwell on the tragedies of the past, but they shaped so much of the city now. And what was important was that he talked, keeping her attention on him and not what was happening around them; the comings and goings of men who'd enter the house and disappear upstairs with their pick of the girls, or sit and smoke in the room with them for a while before disappearing.

Done, Rinn made his excuses, told Pashmira to wait while he has a quiet chat with the madam. She nodded happily enough, relaxed for the first time in his company. It was amazing what a decent bit of food can do. He almost felt guilty about going behind her back and selling her to Covi, but the woman offered good coin and he was happy to pocket it. He didn't owe the girl anything, if she was naïve enough to assume his kindness was anything other than opportunism, well then, more fool her. There is no kindness in Constantinople.

***

Ketus Rinn never came back for her.

"He's been called away," Noe Covi explained, "But he's given me coin to cover your room and board, so follow Sila, she'll show you where you're sleeping. Get your head down. You must be exhausted."

And she was.

Sila was a pretty young girl who dragged her left leg where an accident had left her crippled. Sila led the way, bringing her to a small room high in the roof of the house up four flights of stairs, to a narrow space barely wide enough for the cot and small table with silvered mirror on top of it. "This is yours," the girl said.

It wasn't much, but it was so much more than she'd ever had to call her own before.

Pashmira curled up on the bed.

She hadn't realized just how tired she was.

The next thing she knew, she was being woken Sila, who wanted to know if she wanted to come along with her while she ran some errands, including a trip to the bazaar to buy some fancies for Madam Covi.

Going back was a peculiar thing. She was still new enough to the city to enjoy the excitement of the place, the hubbub of everything happening at once, but it was a different experience this time because everyone knew Sila. They smiled and nodded and took the time to say hello, ask after her mother, the men promising to come by and see her soon. All but one, a shaven-headed man in monk's robes. His name was Nazu Nazis.

Over the first few days at Madam Covi's establishment, Pashmira saw the young monk more than once,
always below stairs.

He wasn't a customer.

The madam had business ties to the monastery.

Over the weeks that followed, waiting for Rinn to
come back for her, Pashmira began to recognize the
faces of some of the gentlemen callers: musicians, a
playwright, fops, and soldiers of rank. She saw Ketus
Rinn twice in those early days, both times bringing a
new girl to the door.

He avoided her every time she ran down the stairs
to see him, disappearing out of the back door even as
she called his name.

After the third time, Sila told her to forget him. He
wasn't who she thought he was. That much was obvious.

But, for all those familiar faces there is one man she
doesn't know anything about.

The vicious, dark, brooding priest who she'd witnessed nearly beat a man to death in the bazaar on her
first day in Constantinople.

She watched him come, but made sure not to be
seen just in case he should recognize her, though his
remembering a slip of a girl from two months ago was
unlikely. She watched him go. He never left with one
of the madam's girls.

That was about to change with a knock on her bedroom door.

It was Madam Covi.

She had a peculiar look on her face. It took Pashmira a moment to realize it was sadness. She wasn't
used to seeing it there. Noe Covi always looked so full
of life. She sat down on the edge of the bed, smoothing
the sheet out beneath her.

"You know what this place is, don't you, child?"

Pashmira nodded.

"Good. That will make this easier. I need you to know I've been good to you, girl. I haven't rushed you, but you can't live in a brothel for free for this long. That's just not the way it works. People are starting to notice. They think I'm playing favorites. You have to start earning her keep. There's a young man waiting for you downstairs, don't disappoint him, girl."

Pashmira didn't say anything as she was led to his room.

Beyond the door, the room was in darkness.

It took her a moment to make out the silhouette of the stranger sitting in a chair in the corner.

"Dance for me, girl," he said. Nothing else. She saw curls of smoke from his pipe, and could smell the sickly sweet tang of hashish in the air. She did as she was told, praying that he wouldn't recognize her. It was strange trying to move her body seductively, swaying without sounds to follow. She felt awkward and ungainly. She wasn't a seductress.

"No," he said eventually, breaking the silence. "Naked. I want to see you move."

Slowly, uncomfortably, Pashmira pulled her thin dress up over her head, exposing her naked body, dreading that moment when he reached out to touch her.

It never came.

He had no interest in her body.

He only wanted to watch her perform.

Pashmira remembered the weapon katas the old man had drilled her in, they were like dances, demanding incredible discipline and close control. She gave herself to the movement as though fighting an invisible foe.

The stranger still didn't move.

For an hour she danced, forcing her body to move faster and faster, muscles cording to offer a shadowy definition, creating a map of valleys and hills out of her flesh, before she collapsed, exhausted, and lay curled on the floor at his feet. Breathing hard. Chest heaving.

The priest rose slowly from his chair. He crossed the room to where she lay, then kicked her once, hard, in the base of the spine. Even as she cried out in pain, he spat on her. "Whore."

He left her there lying on the floor.

Sila found her. She was too sleight to carry her, but even with her deformity, was strong enough to guide Pashmira back up to her room where she huddled, confused and naked until the girl returned with some of her clothes and her mother.

"What did you do girl?"

Pashmira looked at her.

"I told you not to disappoint him," Noe Covi said, her black eyes livid.

"I did everything he asked."

"He wasn't happy. You have one job here, make the man happy." The madam had brought a braided whip with her. She used it on Pashmira. Just the once, a savage lash across the shoulders. "If you ever disappoint an important customer again, I'll use it properly, girl."

The priest returned again the next night, and the night after, first demanding that she read to him, though she had never learned her letters. Because of the light, she saw the distinctive cross he wore around his neck. It was grotesque. The priest punctuated her stumbling explanations that she didn't know the letters with slaps that left stinging red handprints across her face.

Pashmira didn't flinch.

Her lack of response to the pain only served to infuriate the priest all the more. "Whore," he rasped, driving a punch into her gut, brutally hard. The blow doubled her up. A second sent her sprawling across the floor.

He stepped over her and walked out of the room.

This time she didn't lie there helplessly weeping and feeling sorry for herself, she couldn't give in to that weakness. No one was going to save her from this hell she was suddenly living in. She was going to have to save herself. She thought about running away, but knew she wouldn't get far. Everyone knew she was Madam Covi's girl. She needed to get out of Constantinople. And to escape, she needed to know more about the man who hated women so badly he could only stand there impotently, then beat his frustration out on her flesh.

Sila knew who he was; a zealot who loathed all forms of sin and yet frequents brothels, tormenting himself. That was his sickness. "His name is Marwan Azir. You don't want to make an enemy of him. Just do what he says and hope he leaves you alone. That's all anyone can do."

"Not all," Pashmira said, not sure exactly what she could do, only that she couldn't go on having her soul stripped night by night by the vile little man.

The next time he came, Azir demanded Pashmira walk naked through the streets so that he might watch her from afar, unseen.

She refused, but cleverly, not risking the wrath of the madam. She used her head and had Sila bring one of the girls up to her room when she had a few moments. She didn't take much convincing to agree to wear a veil across her face as she ventured out into the streets naked in Pashmira's place. "You owe me," the whore said, offering a mischievous grin. "I'll just have to work out what I want in return," but the way she said it made it obvious what she wanted.

"Just make sure you get his attention," Pashmira said.

"Look at me. Do you really think any man in this city is going to look away?"

As her double walked the prescribed route, drawing hateful glares, and eventually stones from the onlookers, Pashmira scouted the rooftops, moving quickly, keeping low, looking for signs of her tormentor. She knew he had to be there someone, watching. That was what he liked to do. Watch. So she scanned the high windows and rooftops, looking for anywhere that offered an unobstructed view of the route.

It didn't take long to find the priest. He had taken refuge in a shaded sanctuary on one of the rooftops, using a tented roof to keep him out of the sun. It also meant he couldn't see her moving up behind him.

Pashmira ran fleet of foot across the red tiles and the ridges that ran through the center of them like a spine.

The sun was fierce, and she was running out of it.

The priest didn't stand a chance.

Before he could react she had her hand snaked around his neck, body pressed tight up against his back, the point of her curved blade of the Dagger of the Martyrs resting against his ear. "I know who you are, I know where you lay your head at night, I know your sick perversions, I know everything about you, Marwan Azir, and if you don't leave me alone, I will find you while you sleep, and I will cut your miserable impotent little cock off and watch you bleed to death in your bed," she whispered into his ear. "There's a little voyeur in all of us. Do we understand each other?"

"I understand you, whore. But do you understand that you've just signed your death warrant?"

"I don't think so. All I can concentrate on is the stink of piss dribbling down the inside of your leg."

She should have killed him there and then.

She didn't.

That was a mistake.

***

They came in the middle of the night, the girls with their clients.

Eight armored men, Knights of the Cross, led by Marwan Azir.

The priest stood on the doorstep and bellowed out the charges of witchcraft against Pashmira. "Amid your house of filth and sin you harbor a fiend who used magic to displace herself, casting glamors upon her skin to enthrall a good Christian man, driving him out of his mind. Bring the woman out or you all die in the name of God, I swear it so, you *all* die."

Pashmira stood at the window, watching.

"I have to go down there," she told Sila, as the madam's daughter stepped into the room. She turned to see Sila blocking the doorway, shaking her head. "Then what? What am I supposed to do? Hide? You heard him. They'll kill everyone."

"Get out of here. Go. Nazu Nazis is downstairs. He will help you. He is waiting for you. He knows the secret passages of the Basilica Cistern that link the buildings of the Avenue of Princesses. Get out of here. They won't harm us if you aren't here."

Pashmira didn't believe her; men like Marwan Azir didn't hold back when it came to sadistic pleasure. She knew the man better than any of them. She'd been subjected to his perversions and knew the darkness that drove him. He was more of a monster than anything that might come crawling out of the desert.

The sound of fists hammering on the door echoed up the stairs.

"Come on, there's no time. We need to get you away from here."

"Can I trust him?"

"Nazu? With your life."

She did as she was told, taking the servants stairs at the back of the building, the secret passages the girls used when they wanted to move about within the brothel without the eyes of the punters following them.

She hiked up her skirts and ran down the stairs two, three and four at a time, stumbling as the sounds of the front door splintering on its hinges ripped through the panicked brothel.

In seconds the place was in turmoil. She heard screams, and then, sickeningly, an eerie silence followed by the stampede of the knights looking to purge the place.

They were dying up there—and she was running away.

Nazu Nazis waited for her at the false door, face white with fear. "Hurry," he rasped, urging her to duck through the door so that he might seal it again and hide all trace of their passage.

The ground beneath her feet was wet. She splashed

through the dark tunnel, fumbling forward with little light to guide her until Nazu caught up with her carrying the small reed torch in his hand. The tunnel appeared to descend into the Underworld.

"This way," he told Pashmira.

"Where are we going?"

"The passage breaches the Theodosian Wall, taking us out of the city. My monastery lies close to the ruins of the Galata Kulesi ruins to the north of the Golden Horn. We will be safe there."

Pashmira didn't believe that for a moment.

***

For forty-eight hours the wrath of Noe Covi knew no bounds.

Word passed up and down the Avenue of the Princesses: anyone connected to Marwan Azir was to pay for her daughter's death. Soldiers, associates, friends, anyone Marwan believed he could trust, was fair game.

He was poison; his people a cancer to be cut out of Byzantine society.

And of course they came to the pleasure houses and bathhouses looking for release, that would never change. Men were men, powerful men more corrupt and venal than most. They looked at sex as their divine right, at the girls as nothing more than whores to be bought, and never imagined what they were lying down beside.

Fifty corpses were tossed into the harbor as Covi looked for justice.

But Marwan Azir himself, and his guard of zealots, remained elusive.

She couldn't get to him with her army of whores.

***

Pashmira disguised herself as a novitiate, shaved, dressed, strapped down so her body didn't betray her sex.

"No one must know you are a women," the Abbot said. "You shouldn't even be here. You will be the death of us all. Marwan Azir is insane. He will not rest until you are dead. But, if you swear to lead the humble life of a novitiate, rising for the prayers, tending the roses in the garden, and devoting your life to God, then we shall hide you here for as long as we can." The inference being it couldn't be forever. She understood that.

And for a few days she did find a peace of sorts in the simple chores that made up daily life in this house of God. But it was a fragile peace. Despite the humility of these men, one man viewed her with extreme skepticism. His name was Akerios. A Greek. It didn't take her long to realize this was because of a deep-seated hatred for Nazu. She felt his eyes on her at all times, watching her, waiting for her to make a mistake.

And she did, of course. It was inevitable that she would. She couldn't bathe with the brothers, she was more delicate, and struggled with their scholarly devotions. She stumbled over the prayers. Nothing about her could hold up to close scrutiny. But even once he'd worked out her secret she could never have expected what happened. She wanted to believe the blood was on his hands. But it wasn't. Not all of it. If she hadn't been there the monks would have been alive, just as her presence had brought death to the whorehouse.

On his next errand behind the Theodosian wall into the city proper, Akerios went in search of the zealot

Marwan Azir, and sold Pashmira out. Marwan's knights came to the monastery, and in less than an hour butchered everyone, including Nazu and the man who had sold her out, Akerios. She labored over their burials, weeping as she helped send the men on the way to their god.

Even if she had wanted to, she couldn't stay here now.

This wasn't her home.

She was a creature of war.

She was at home with death.

Now that blood had been spilled in the shrine, the sanctuary was defiled forever.

The city was no place for her. Not as long as the zealot still lived. She needed to kill him or leave, and it would be easier to find a caravan to travel the Spice Road than it would be to get away with murder.

But she had learned one thing about herself: she wasn't one for doing things the easy way.

Pashmira returned to the Cistern, walking through the passages close to the brothel, listening to the splash of water, searching out the network of tunnels that would lead her out to the aqueduct that still carried water from the Belgrad forest into the dilapidated fortress of the Sacred Palace where Marwan Azir's holy army had made their camp.

The waterway offered a silent entry into the very heart of their encampment.

Pashmira sank into the water, swimming silently across the huge aqueduct, focused on a single act of vengeance. She didn't care about failure. Failure only meant dying. That wasn't such a bad fate. The water cooled as she swam, day turning to night, leeching the water of its heat.

She emerged, dripping wet, the Dagger of the Martyrs between her teeth, the moon at her back, and moved like a ghost from building to building, room to room, in search of Marwan.

There was no one around.

No guards posted to watch for threats from the City.

That was the arrogance of the holy man; he believed himself untouchable.

She was about to change all of that.

Up ahead she heard movement. Footsteps.

Pashmira pressed herself up against the wall, willing the shadows to fold around her. She saw him; one of Marwan's men. She recognized him from the market place and again from the slaughter at the whorehouse. He had been on the steps behind Marwan Azir as he read his proclamation.

She waited, unmoving, as he came towards her.

He couldn't see her.

She slipped out of the shadows, pressing the blade up against his throat, "You should pick your friends more carefully," she whispered in his ear as the knight's back stiffened. "You have a choice, silence and life, make a sound and die. Which is it to be?"

The knight shook his head.

Pashmira didn't worry about moral implications or where her soul was going. She had been damned from the moment she stepped off that boat. She sliced the blade cleaning across his throat and held him in place as he gurgled into death.

Only then did she lay him aside as if sleeping, and continued her search until she found the priest's chamber.

Marwan Azir was asleep, curled up on a cot, a single blanket drawn up to his chin.

She crossed the room to where he lay.

He didn't look like the devil.

He didn't look like death.

And yet he was both and he was so much more besides.

She thought for a moment about simply killing him, but there was no satisfaction in that. She wanted him to know *why* he is dying and *who* it was offering him up to Hell.

Like some black-hearted angel of death descending on him, she woke him by forcing open his jaw and cutting out his tongue before he could raise the alarm. Blood as black as his soul pooled in his mouth. He bucked and thrashed beneath her weight, but she wasn't about to let him wriggle free.

"I might be a whore," she said coldly, "But you are a ghost."

Slowly, enjoying the moment, she drew the knife's blade across his sternum, opening him up, like a flower from the monk's garden coming into bloom. "That was for my friend, Sila." She carried on with the cut, all the way down to the rise of his cock, an inch deep, the slice accompanied by gurgling screams. "And that is for Nazu." And with each fresh slice she explained who the wounds were for. The monks, the whores, the old man in the market place.

She didn't let him go gently, but he went just the same.

When Marwan Azir was finally dead she took the zealot's crucifix from around his neck, a gift she intended to give to another Sister of War.

***

CRUSADER KINGS II: TALES OF TREACHERY

The brothel was quiet. There were no lights in any of the windows along the Avenue of Princesses. Noe Covi sat in a chair in the dark. She was alone. Pashmira walked into the parlor where she had first met the woman. A lot had happened in what felt like such a short time. She wasn't the innocent girl she had been when she followed Ketus Rinn to the whorehouse.

"What are you doing here, girl?" The madam asked.

Pashmira didn't say anything.

She crossed the room and put Marwan Azir's crucifix in the grieving woman's hand.

"The man who murdered your daughter is dead."

Covi looked at her, seeing Pashmira properly for the first time.

"Who *are* you?"

"No one. A Sister of War."

"More will come. You do know that, don't you? You can't kill a man like Azir without someone wanting to take revenge."

Pashmira nodded.

"What do you intend to do?"

"Leave."

The madam nodded. "I can help with that. Rest. No one will look for you here. I will find someone to get you out of the city. Live, girl. That is the only way to win against these men. Live."

"I intend to."

She slept in her old room one last time, thinking of the life she might have had.

Come first light Pashmira headed out to find the caravan master who would take her out of the city.

He had his back to her, but she knew who it was.

Ketus Rinn.

He turned.

"It seems we have come full circle," he said, seeing her approach. He smiled, doing his utmost not to seem rattled by the identity of his passenger.

"I don't think so. I'm not your whore to sell." She held up her hand, letting the man see the rust-colored smear on her palm. "Do you know what this is?" He nodded. "Just to be sure, his name was Marwan Azir. He couldn't even beg for salvation at the end. I saw to that. Don't think I'm some sweet little girl for you to exploit, Ketus. You made me. Remember that."

"Full circle," he said.

And in a way it was, at least for her.

She needed him, just as she had on her first day in the city.

She was in his hands.

There was one difference this time.

She had blood on her hands and he knew it.

***

IN ACTUAL HISTORY

In the days leading up to the fall of the city, Constantinople--a thriving hub of civilisation that had already survived the Black Death and one change of identity--was a key piece in the geopolitical puzzle of East and West. Tensions were riding high, from the slave markets all the way to the Hagia Sophia. The Christian forces had used the city as a staging post for centuries, building dazzling forums and the Church of the Holy Apostles to cement their seat of power, but the peace was uneasy. War was coming. Three days of pillage and plunder and deconsecration would follow, and the city as it was could never be the same again as the age of the Ottoman Empire was ushered in. Mehmed II gathered forces outside the Golden Horn, preparing to converge upon the city while the slavers, whoremasters and silk merchants went about their business wilfully ignorant of the threat. Knights patrolled the streets, priests decried the heathen infidels, creating enemies among the faithful. There was a constant undercurrent of fear and expectancy. The peace could not hold...

ABOUT STEVEN SAVILE

Steven Savile has written for *Doctor Who, Torchwood, Primeval, Stargate, Warhammer, Slaine, Fireborn, Pathfinder* and other popular game and comic worlds. His novels have been published in eight languages to date, including the Italian bestseller *L'eridita*. He won the International Media Association of Tie-In Writers award for his *Primeval* novel, *Shadow of the Jaguar*, published by Titan, in 2010, and has been nominated for the British Fantasy Award on multiple occasions. *Silver*, his debut thriller reached #2 in the Amazon UK e-charts in the summer of 2011 selling over 75,000 copies worldwide.

A POMERANIAN TALE

By Cory Lachance

Excerpted from Bram Stoker's *The Voivode*

Dear Professor,

Once again I offer you my most profuse gratitude for your lesson on the language and customs of the Wendish folk, as despite its sadly necessary brevity it has already proven immensely useful to me on this first leg of my visit to the Empire. I write to you now in the dead of night from a small village with a name most unpronounceable to English tongues, when I ought to be sleeping—or at least reviewing documents in preparation for the meeting with my client, the Voivode— because I wish to share with you, while it is still fresh in my mind, a remarkable tale from the local folklore which was recited to me earlier this eve amidst unusual circumstances.

To set the scene, I will first explain how I arrived

here. The journey by sea from London to Gdansk was pleasantly uneventful, and the same could be said of the journey by train from Gdansk to Slawno. I must say that the portrait you painted of this land, with its bustling port towns and idyllic countryside replete with rivers, lakes, and forests of unmatched splendour was delightfully accurate. Less delightful was your description of the social realities; indeed, in my observations of these people I have recalled your assertion that the Wendish Empire has stagnated on the world stage precisely because its reactionary nobility have failed to acknowledge the Enlightenment which has scoured the darkness of ignorance and tyranny from the rest of Europe. The many tribulations the Wends have faced have made them paranoid of outside influence, but at the cost of national progress. What does it matter to the indentured serf whether his yoke is held by heathen Tartar or brother Slav?

But I digress. From Slawno I hired a carriage to take me south to the castle of the Voivode. The journey was estimated to take three days, but the weather grew ever more foul the further inland we travelled and our pace slowed accordingly. Finally the driver stopped in this village and proclaimed that he would go no further until tomorrow. I became annoyed at being delayed further, as by my estimation we could still reach the castle by nightfall, even with the rain. He refused my entreaties and explained the possibility of getting stuck in the mud, and that under no circumstances would he risk being trapped in the night between the village and the castle. This baffled me, and when he mentioned that he knew of a public house in town where I could stay, I became enraged, assuming this to be the establishment of some cousin or other of his, and this whole business to be a ruse intended to bilk me, another stupid foreigner in their eyes, of a few more shillings, and I made my suspicions known to him in words admittedly unbecoming of a gentleman. Imagine my surprise, then, when he arranged my stay with the proprietor out of his own meagre pocket!

With nothing else to be done, I ate and drank with the village men, and struck up a friendly conversation with the local magistrate, a somewhat learned fellow who spoke with me in surprisingly excellent—if a tad archaic—English. The appeal of the Bard is far-reaching. When I told him of the carriage-driver's bizarre behaviour, he laughed and told me that the superstitious common folk in these parts believe that old King Jozef's ghost still haunts the castle, and sends wolves and bats into the night to kill for his pleasure. At the mention of King Jozef an old man, with eyes yellowed by cataracts and the great swollen red nose of the habitual drunkard, rose from his seat in the corner and began shouting in our direction.

"Here is a prime example," the magistrate said to me. "Zbigniew here would like to tell you the tale of King Jozef's death, passed down in his family for centuries, and I pray you will listen, because when he gets all fired up, he always ruins the mood of this establishment until he gets his way. I will translate for you."

I assented, and the tale was told to me as follows.

***

In the days before the Empire, in the Kingdom of Old Pomerania, Jozef the Bastard, Jozef the Usurper, Jozef the Cruel, the Impaler, the Heretic, the Beast, son of the Dragon of Revelation, son of the Devil, scoured the land in a reign of terror lasting two score and two years after wrenching the crown from the rightful king, his half-brother Gryn II, with an army of rapacious sell-swords and bandits. All lived in terror then, for no family, common nor gentle, was safe from robbery and murder or worse at the hands of the king's men, for Jozef the Wanton delighted so in misery and destruction, and was said to torture prisoners by the hundreds in the dungeon of his impregnable fortress.

As for Prince Gryn, the true king by all the laws of God and man, he was kept under house arrest in Weligrad, and Jozef plied him with all manner of liquor and wenches and sedating herbs, ensuring his complacency through the satisfaction of his sinful weaknesses. That Gryn still lived was the only mercy ever shown by Jozef, and would prove by fate to be his greatest regret.

For after twenty-two years of unspeakable atrocities, St. Eckhart the Good German, who by the grace of God had succeeded many years past in his mission to convert King Gryn I and his subjects to the veneration of Christ, returned once more to this land in order to save the souls of its people. The wise and elderly priest, now frail of body but still sharp of mind, was spirited into the erstwhile Gryn II's chambers, and there found the prince in a melancholic stupor.

"Lo, what times are these, else they are the end times, that the son and scion of the noblest man that ever I knew should be reduced to such a fat and wallowing state, whilst his ill-begotten heretic brother lays low his birthright and makes war against Christ?" lamented Eckhart.

At the sound of that blessed martyr's voice, the prince stirred at last from the hazy waking dream which had gripped him for so long.

"Eckhart? God grant mercy! Are you not exiled on my brother's order? How and wherefore have you returned to this accursed kingdom?"

"Have you not heard, even locked away in this tower, how your bastard brother has been excommunicated by the Holy Father, and the whole of Pomerania placed under interdict for his vile deeds? His iron grip loosens, Gryn. He has betrayed his every ally, squandered all his stolen riches, and defaulted on every contract and agreement which helped to sustain his power. Yet a shadow still falls across the land. I saw myself how an evil comet streaked across the northern sky, and have heard how nocturnal beasts savage the country, and how the mass is said backwards at midnight over the bodies of naked women in the churches your father built, and how satyrs stalk the woods seducing the maidenhead from peasant virgins. The omens are there, Gryn, and have been since your wretched brother's birth: he is Anti-Christ, and if the soul of this country is to be saved, it must be now, and by you, ordained as the representative on Earth of God's just rule in Heaven, the king."

And Gryn wept pitifully then, and kissed Eckhart's ring again and again and begged the Lord for forgiveness for allowing such evil to hold sway for so long over his kingdom, and for failing to resist the endless temptations showered on him in the name of the Devil's work. The holy Saint bade him rise, and together they made their escape from Weligrad, and gathered unto them all the abused and disgruntled lords of the realm and fomented a glorious rebellion against the Usurper. There were many terrible battles fought, and though much blood was spilt and lives lost, the Lord was with Gryn and Eckhart, and He granted them victory after victory until only the mighty castle of Jozef yet stood between them and the fulfilment of their righteous cause.

Alas, the walls of the fortress proved unbreachable, and a long siege followed. Gryn's camp was afflicted first with the pox, then dysentery, and then all other manner of diseases and indignities. Winter came unnaturally early and it was the coldest and darkest occurrence of that season in a lifetime, and many of Gryn's men froze to death in their tents. The ground too was frozen solid, so the men could not be buried properly, and a cloud of ravens flew perpetually overhead, engorging themselves on the veritable feast of carrion thus provided. The prince cried out to the Lord, asking why He had forsaken them.

"Do not disparage, Gryn," Eckhart counselled, "for the Lord is ever with the honourable and good. No, these evils that beset us issue forth from the Adversary, and God will deliver us from them, if you pray He do so, and do not take His name in vain!"

He was proven right when, on All Hallow's Eve, a malnourished servant boy from the castle was brought before the prince.

"My lord, I have come to you at great risk to myself and to my family, for I believe that allowing this siege to continue would be a greater risk to all. Whatever hardships you have suffered out here, the same have been visited upon us. The King has made all within the castle his prisoners for fear of mutiny, and he hoards all supplies and allows us servants to starve so that only he and his retainers are kept fed. He flays alive any whom he suspects of treason. As my grandfather lay dying of hunger, he whispered to me with his last breath of a secret passage in the throne room, by which I might escape at night, which leads through many dark and treacherous tunnels to a hidden exit on the outer walls. I can bring you there, and show you the way through, so that a number of you might infiltrate the castle and open the gate, and end this horrible war. Please, my lord, make haste! I fear for my father and mother, lest my absence be discovered."

Gryn thanked God for bestowing deliverance upon him and resolved that, since he sought absolution for his sin of inaction, he and his cadre of bodyguards would be the ones to undertake the dangerous task. Eckhart joined too, despite the prince's protests, explaining that if the Evil One truly had his baleful eye trained on the castle, then a man of God must be present to combat his influence. So they skirted the lofty walls until they came to the secret door, and the boy led them into the dark and confining halls. Through a twisting labyrinth, into the caverns beneath the castle wherein devious shadows hid perilous chasms of unknown depth, and back up into the central keep of the citadel the prince and his companions trod. When they came to a hall with an apparent dead end, the boy pressed upon a certain stone, and a portion of the wall opened by a hidden mechanism. The party crept into the apparently empty throne room, and as they crossed it attempted to maintain utter silence, until Gryn felt a drop of liquid fall onto his face. Wiping it with his glove, he saw that it was red, and swung his torch up to find the source. There, suspended from the highest ceiling arch, was a barred cage, and in it slumped the bodies of a man and woman with their throats slit, their dead eyes staring down at him.

"Mama! Papa!" the servant boy cried. One of

Gryn's men moved to stifle the boy's wailing, but it was too late. The pounding of armoured boots on stone floors echoed from the adjoining rooms, and the prince's company was soon surrounded by half-again as many men of Jozef's guard. The Usurper himself entered, training a loaded crossbow on the distraught lad.

"Little mouse!" he taunted. "For delivering my treasonous brother into my grasp, I must prepare you a suitable reward. Your parents have already reaped theirs, as you can see."

"Monster!" said Eckhart. "How dare you make light of heinous murder. The stain of countless mortal sins is upon you, and you will laugh no more when the lake of fire sears your flesh forevermore."

"Aha!" said Jozef. "Here we have the serpent who whispered into my dear brother's ear, convincing him to abandon paradise for doomed revolution! Tell me, old man, how fares your conscience to witness the death and misery your lies have wrought?"

Gryn bristled at the affront to the holiest man then alive.

"Speak not of conscience, half-brother, when so many crimes are upon your head. Eckhart brought the light of Christ to our people, a legacy you have made every attempt to destroy, but as of yet have failed, and ever will."

"It was not the false theology of this foolish old German, whatever he may claim, that changed the heart of our cowardly father, but the points of Danish swords! He feared for his own life, and betrayed the old ways in order to preserve it, rather than face defeat like a true warrior. Krutoj built this kingdom on Christian blood, when he killed Gottschalk and sent his sons scurrying to Denmark, and strengthened it further by bringing battle to all the enemies of Pomerania to honour the gods of the Slavs. Blood is the heart of Pomerania, and it is for the return of that glorious legacy that I took the crown, when you would not relinquish it. I have paid you just recompense all these years, have I not? Betrayal is all this poisonous missionary has ever preached, and the ruin of our realm is his greatest desire."

"Guard your heart against falsehood, Gryn," warned Eckhart. "The father of lies speaks through him, for he is his son if anyone is! He knows he has already lost. What a bitter farce, that he is the first of his line to receive a Christian name, and blasphemes with every word against the Lord whose foster father was his namesake. He speaks spuriously of faith in Christ as ruinous while endorsing the sacrifice of innocent babes to feed Czernobog's hunger."

The prince's weakness began to show once more as the priest and the Usurper argued back and forth. Uncertainty took hold in his heart, where embers of the love he had borne his brother when they were children still smoldered, and his courage shrank away as the two titans hurled insults and all the warriors moved their hands to their scabbards in preparation for the inevitable outbreak of violence. Jozef, spying doubt in Gryn's countenance, made him one last entreaty.

"Brother, I would spare your life again, if only you will surrender and hand me over the priest to be tried and burned as the prime agent of the rebellion. You may return to Weligrad unmolested, and there I will double the luxuries I have afforded you thus far. You will have the finest spiced wines and rarest liqueurs, the most sumptuous feasts of venison hunted in my royal forests. Nubile courtesans will tend to your every desire, and I will even share with you my wives, the most beautiful women who have ever walked the earth."

Then three women of unmatched fairness and exotic elegance emerged from the shadows and approached the prince, and ran their hands over his face and body, before disrobing from their nightclothes, and they tickled—

—Here the magistrate whispered to me that he would spare me the details of this, Zbigniew's favourite part of the tale to recount, as he could see I was already blushing like a true Englishman. Suffice it to say, he said, that the women are described as such that could tempt any man to mortal sin. I could tell by how the old man's eyes bulged, how he flared his nostrils and lashed his tongue lecherously about, that he was picturing this scene quite vividly as he spoke—

—"God help me," Gryn said, his knees wobbling. "I only want peace, and they are so fair and tender and kind."

"Steel yourself, my lord!" Eckhart admonished. "Be they witches or succubi, these three are masters of the dark arts, having travelled from the far corners of the world to incite your brother to madness. I remember their faces well: twenty years ago they advised him to banish me from his court and kingdom. They have not aged a day since then. Bathing in the blood of virgins sustains their counterfeit youth!"

But the lustful prince was mesmerized under the women's enchantment and could say or do nothing more, and the Usurper's men advanced upon him. Then the Lord inspired St. Eckhart the Good German, who produced a philtre of holy water he had secreted on his person, and he splashed it upon the alluring witches. The power of Christ cast down their wicked glamour, and they fell to the ground and howled in terror as their true visages were revealed. When Gryn saw that the irresistible trio were in fact twisted hags with milky eyes and warty limbs the spell was finally lifted from his mind; alas, it was not in time to save the blessed martyr Eckhart, who was struck in the chest with a bolt from Jozef's crossbow.

The two sides engaged and a chaotic melee erupted in the throne room, where the roaring clash of swords and shields became deafening. Although the prince was outnumbered, he was also possessed by a mad grief for having let his friend die, which drove him full wroth and he struck down many more than his share of Jozef's knights. The last few of the Usurper's men fled in terror when they beheld Gryn's fury, leaving the false king to his fate. Jozef was thrown at Gryn's feet.

"Please, brother!" he whimpered. "I spared your life once out of love. For the sake of our father's memory, would you not do the same? I know I have wronged you and I repent my sins. I will do whatever you ask, if you will only let me live!"

"For the sake of our father's memory, Jozef, I, with the power invested in me as the rightful king of Pomerania, find you guilty of high treason and heresy, and hereby sentence you to death."

With his own sword, Gryn cut the head off his only brother, ending at last the brutal reign of Pomerania's most sadistic monarch. He and his men hastened to the castle gate and opened it, allowing his army to pour in and make quick work of the remaining defenders. As for the orphaned servant boy, Gryn made him his squire, and years later knighted him for his service and sacrifice. Eckhart was canonized and eventually sainted in light of his pivotal role in bringing the kingdom into the fold of the One Holy Church. The three witches were burned at the stake after a formal inquisition, but Gryn could not bring himself to immolate his brother's body. In one last act of weakness, he had Jozef buried on church lands after a proper funeral. The grave was found empty three days later--it is said that the consecrated ground could not accept so evil a man in its embrace.

***

With that the old man settled down and everyone returned to their drinks and previous conversations.

"So you see," said the magistrate, "why your driver would wish to avoid the castle. Every man in these parts knows this story by heart, since Zbigniew recounts it so often, whenever or wherever he can. Parents frighten their children, telling them that bad King Jozef will eat them if they wander too far at night, and most are simple enough to believe it even into adulthood. The history books are vague and dry on this matter, while this tale fires something in the imagination of us Pomeranian Wends."

I thanked the magistrate for his insight, and upon retiring to my room began immediately to compose this letter to you. It would seem my imagination has been fired as well. I had heard the Christianization of this realm was turbulent, but I am shocked to find echoes of that time still resounding in the hearts of modern men.

I think when the Voivode comes to London I shall

endeavour to arrange a meeting between the two of you. I envision it might be quite fruitful. I believe there is always a grain of truth in even the most fanciful fables, and if even a fraction of the horrible events from the tale I have just heard truly occurred in the Voivode's current home, then I must infer that his curiosity must be of that morbid sort that you and I share as well, especially considering his impending purchase of Quetzalcoatl Hall, where as you know even ghastlier atrocities took place in our own country's darkest period.

It is only a few scant hours until dawn now, when I shall resume my travel. I hope my dreams shan't be too haunted.

Yours Sincerely,
Jonathan Harker, Solicitor

***

IN ACTUAL HISTORY

"A Pomeranian Tale" is framed as an excerpt from an alternate history's version of the novel Dracula, in which a peasant of the Wendish Empire tells Jonathan Harker the story of a legendary usurper king whose reign of terror and eventual defeat was the defining epoch of that country's formative medieval period. Centuries of fantastical embellishment have seemingly obfuscated the real events of that time, but the unwitting Harker may come closer to the truth than he ever could have foreseen.

ABOUT CORY LACHANCE

Cory Lachance is an aspiring writer and musician from Victoria, British Columbia, Canada, who could probably cease aspiring and achieve his ambitions if it weren't for the frankly embarrassing number of hours he has logged in *Crusader Kings II*.

Cory Lachance is one of the winners of the *Crusader Kings II* Short Story Contest 2014.

THE CHILDREN'S CRUSADE

By Jordan Ellinger

In the early morning of the last day of summer the Lord our God caused a mist to arise on the sea outside of Jaffa. When it receded, He revealed to us thirty ships which had carried the warriors of the Children's Crusade to the shores of the Holy Land.

They made landfall a few miles down the coast, possibly, guessed Allah li-Din al-Nasir, to avoid the city's naval defenses. I had my doubts, and those doubts were confirmed when we met them on the beach with a small group of soldiers at our back.

"Are we in the Holy Land, good sir?" asked a small blond boy in German. Barefoot and dressed in rags, he looked like he hadn't eaten a single meal for the length of his voyage across the Mediterranean. I estimated his age at twelve and he was one of the oldest of the group of perhaps a dozen children who waded through the surf towards us. Their vessel, nothing more than a fishing scow, had beached itself a few feet from the shore.

He had seen the red cross of a Knight Templar on

my rather ill-fitting armour, but as his gaze took in my escort he began to pale. The Saracens have always been a dark-skinned race and not as fond of armour as good Christian knights. It was obvious to the boy that he faced a well-armed enemy, and he shouted in alarm as he ran back towards his friends.

One of the Saracens lifted his crossbow, but al-Nasir waved it down. The Caliph was a slight, scholarly man with a well-trimmed beard and unblemished skin. He spoke softly at all times because he believed that a man will pay attention to what he strains to hear. "Would you fire on a child, Siraf?"

Though al-Nasir's tone had been almost philosophical, Siraf bowed his head. Nasir looked at me. "What do you make of this, Sir Nevsky? As a Christian?"

As educated as he was, al-Nasir still tended to think of Christians as a single ethnic group. Thus, because I too was a Christian, albeit one who'd lived in the Holy Land for most of his life, it was up to me to divine the motivations of these children.

"They could be escaped slaves who have either commandeered their vessel or killed the slavers who sailed it. But while that might explain one, or even two ships, it cannot explain thirty. They are armed, but though the oldest among them might fight in the army of a particularly desperate noble, even the youngest carries a dagger." I removed my helmet. "By your leave, I would like to locate their leader and ask him myself."

Al-Nasir nodded slightly. Through some unspoken mechanism that only great leaders possess, he indicated that Siraf should accompany me and we kicked our steeds into a canter that took us up the beach, past a line of stranded ships. Everywhere, children scattered before us. At last, we came to a large vessel that the retreating tide had left sitting on its side. Here there was a large group of older children and some young men. The tallest amongst them drew his sword and approached us with the others trailing behind him.

He was tall and lean, though not uncomfortably so, like some of the waifs we had encountered on our way here. His hair was so filthy I could not discern its color and his hair was cut raggedly, as if by a kitchen knife. His cheeks bore the shadow of a boy not quite ready to shave. Despite his poor appearance, he carried himself with the ferocious confidence only a zealot can muster, and when he spoke I could tell at once that he was a master orator.

"I had expected to find Christian knights in the Holy Land, but fighting against the Saracens, not at their side," he said, looking from me to Siraf.

"My name is Sir Robert Nevksy of Laufenthal," I said, reminding him that, though we may be in Saracen lands, good Christian manners should not be forgotten, "To whom am I speaking?"

The boy flushed. "Nicholas of Cologne. I have been commanded by God to lead the children of Europe on a new Crusade to free the Holy Land from the Moslem. Our Lord commands that you too set aside your allegiances and join us."

"I'm not in the service of the Caliph and thus have nothing to set aside. I work for the Templars as a banker. Christian missionaries deposit their funds with us in Europe and I dispense it back to them once they reach Jaffa. I am here because al-Nasir received reports of ships full of children crossing the sea and invited me to accompany him on what he thought was a humanitarian mission. We have brought food for you to eat and clothes for you to wear."

A small blond boy dashed up to Nicholas and glanced sternly at me before whispering in the larger boy's ear. I could not overhear the message, but a smile creased the child general's face upon hearing it. It was not a nice smile.

"It seems that our Lord was right to send children in the place of men. Our soldiers surprised a group of infidels and slaughtered them." A ragged cheer arose from the children around him that surged in volume once Nicholas indicated with a hand motion that they should display more enthusiasm. He turned back to me. "Because you are a Christian, I will allow you to leave. Go to Jaffa and tell them to throw open their gates to the righteous army of God and they will be saved."

I left his company in haste, worried for the fate of the Caliph. Minutes later, we came upon a scene of carnage where I'd left him. Dead children, some as young as eight or nine years of age, lay face down in the sand alongside the bodies of grown men. Blood was everywhere. Some of the combatants remained, boys who stared through us as we passed, still reeling from their first exposure to the horrors of war. I felt sadness for them and a sudden intense hatred for Nicholas of Cologne. He was the pie-eyed piper who'd driven these boys to their death. Certainly he'd triumphed here, but even a single Saracen brigade would wipe them out. It was up to me to save them from themselves.

When we did not find the Caliph's body, we pressed on to Jaffa and there learned that he had taken an arrow in his midriff, but was expected to recover. I begged to be allowed an audience and one was granted.

The Caliph rose from his bed to greet me, and though he moved gingerly, he assured me that the loss of his men pained him more than his wound. Once we'd performed the customary greetings and abasements necessitated by our stations, he sat at a table made from European oak left over from when the first Crusaders had ruled the Holy Land and motioned for his servants to bring us some refreshments.

"With respect, your Eminence, what do you intend to do about the Child Army?" I asked.

He took a date from a golden bowl and bit into it. His dark eyes studied mine for some time before he spoke. "I can always tell when a man is asking me a question he has already answered in his own mind, Sir Nevsky."

I cleared my throat, sensing that I'd misstepped. The Caliph was a civilized man, but brutal when he needed to be, and when I spoke again it was difficult not to stutter. "When I was very young, there was a drought that killed most of the crops near the village that my father owned. Only one farm was left untouched. Perhaps there was an underground stream nearby, but for whatever reason, this man's yields were greater than normal that year. Word began to circulate among the peasants that Rudger, for that was his name, had been touched by God and when the village priest, no more educated than the others, proclaimed that it was so, he began to believe. He got it into his head that, because God love him so, he should rule in the place of my father, and he encouraged the other peasants to take up arms against us. My father had always been a just and benevolent ruler, and he did everything he could to try and placate the rebels, to no avail.

"Like Child Army, the men who attacked my father's castle that night with nothing but hammers and pitchforks believed that God was on their side, and they were slaughtered to a man. I have no wish to see that tragedy repeated. Give me three days and I will convince the children in Nicholas' army to lay down their arms."

The caliph regarded me stonily, betraying nothing. He adjusted his position, as if the wound in his side pained him.

"My father, too, was a wise man," he said at last. "We have that in common. He told me that a wise ruler must tread a line between what is right and what is just. It is just that I grant you your three days, but after that, I will do what is right."

Nicholas' rag tag army arrived at the gates outside the city a day later. Curious townsfolk climbed the city walls to get a look at this so-called divine army. There were fewer than two thousand soldiers under his command and his forces looked tiny compared to the mighty battlements that they besieged.

I waited for them outside the gates with only a few men at my side. Behind us was a large tent that my men and I had pitched overnight. I felt that I knew Nicholas because I'd known Rudger. Both had fed on the admiration of their supporters. With the help of the device inside that tent, I hoped to deprive him of that.

Nicholas rode out to meet me on horses he'd stolen from the Saracens that he'd killed. Several of the eldest children followed close behind him, none older than sixteen.

"Has the Lord convinced you to join our cause?" he asked. He had not even bothered to clean the blood off his armor and his face was smeared with mud, but he was so convinced that he was on the side of Right that his question was asked honestly.

"Last night, I prayed for guidance from the Lord,

and He sent an angel to relay this message to you: lay down your arms and act as the Lamb did, not as the Lion."

Nicholas darkened like a storm. "I doubt that God would relay a message to me through you. When the Lord speaks, He speaks to me directly."

I had anticipated this response and had an answer ready. "The angel knew that you would have your doubts, so He promised that He would appear to you and your lieutenants in person to prove the veracity of my claims. Come with me, and He will manifest himself before you."

A true charlatan might have agreed instantly, knowing that such a miracle was impossible. To his credit, Nicholas waffled. He could not be seen to be reluctant to meet an angel in front of his lieutenants, but what if the angel contradicted him? In the end though, he had no choice. If he refused, he would face a rebellion.

We returned with Nicholas and his lieutenants to the city gates. The townsfolk had been cleared off the walls and archers stood in their place. I stole a glance at the child general but he was calm, as only fanatics can be. We approached the tent my men and I had set up last night and dismounted.

The inside was empty and the only light inside came from the opened flap. There was a moment of complete darkness when I closed it that was nearly our undoing. Before an assistant could open the small hole in the back of the tent that let in a shaft of light, one of Nicholas's lieutenants had drawn his sword and lunged for the nearest Saracen.

"Look there!" I shouted, and all movement ceased.

A shaft of light from the hole lit up the far side of the tent, and on the canvas surface was a strange image.

A knight in shining armour galloped towards us, except that everything was inverted so that it looked like his horse's hooves touched the sky and his helmet brushed the earth. I hoped that Nicholas and his boy soldiers would be so distracted by the sight that they wouldn't notice that the sound of hoofbeats was coming from behind them, and not from the image itself.

One of the boys muttered something in an unfamiliar dialect and another fell to his knees as the image of the knight grew and grew until it dominated the inside of the tent, looming before us like a giant. Its horse snorted steam and its hooves pawed the sky. Though I knew this to be no miracle, or rather a miracle of optics, I too found it difficult to suppress my awe. Had I not known that the image of a knight outside the tent was being projected inside via the *camera obscura*, I too might have fallen to my knees.

On my signal, the circular flap was replaced and the tent was once again plunged into darkness. One of the boys sobbed in the back. By the time I returned Nicholas and his soldiers to their army I felt certain that I had scored a victory from which he could never recover.

I changed my mind the next morning. Three giant crucifixes had been raised near the centre of the army upon which tiny bodies had been hung. Al-Nasir leaned against the battlements on folded arms, dressed in a long white robe.

"My chancellor outlined your plan to me this morning. Your requirements are...extensive," he said without removing his gaze from the army.

"I can see no other way of extricating you from the trap that has been sprung, Your Eminence," I said.

Al-Nasir pushed away from the battlements and

snapped his fingers absently as he turned towards me. A nearby servant dashed up and draped the skin of a white tiger around his shoulders.

"You believe this invasion is nothing more than a ruse?" he asked, his interest piqued. It was too his credit that he took me seriously, even though I hadn't seem a day of combat since my youth and had never had much of a grasp on battlefield tactics.

"I am convinced of it. Nicholas of Cologne could not have arranged all this himself. Somewhere, there is a European lord hoping for a slaughter of innocents." I indicated the army with a gauntleted hand. "If word gets back to the Christian world that you slaughtered two thousand children you'll have a million angry knights on your doorstep before Year's End."

His eyes narrowed. "And would you be the one to make sure word gets back to the Christian world?"

"You misunderstand my meaning," I stuttered and then added a quick "your Eminence. The Lords of Europe have been told that the infidels who occupy the Holy Lands eat babies for breakfast. They're counting on savages to act savagely. Please. Disappoint them."

"You are dismissed, Sir Nevsky," said the Caliph. A dangerous tone had crept into his voice, and I wondered what I'd said wrong. Despite my lack of combat experience, I knew enough about etiquette to vanish when I was ordered to do so and I quickly descended the battlements to the front gate.

This time, I went to the child army unaccompanied by any Saracens. I passed through ranks of dirty, stinking children to the centre of the camp. There, Nicholas had erected a pavilion that he'd claimed as spoils from the battle at the beach. His lieutenants were heavily armed, and though the armour they wore was ill-fitting, it was hard to find them comical. Their faces were thin, their cheeks sunken by starvation, and their eyes had a hollow, desperate look to them.

"Here comes the great deceiver," the child general said as I entered the pavilion, "fresh from his devil's trickery." He rose from the pile of silk cushions on which he sat and indicated the other boys in the tent. "None of us were fooled by your little display. We are united before God and we will take Jaffa in his name."

"You are only united because you crucified any dissenters," I said bitterly.

"They should be grateful to die in the same manner as our Lord Jesus Christ," he answered with a shrug.

"Our Lord was a righteous man executed by unbelievers. Are you comparing their suffering to His?"

Nicholas blinked, having not seen the trap until he'd walked into it. He began to choke out a defence of his actions, more for the benefit of his lieutenants than for me, but I cut him off. "The Caliph begs your favour. He asks that either you, or men of your choosing, meet him inside the city to discuss the terms under which the coming battle will be fought."

Of course the Caliph had done no such thing, and judging from our conversation on the battlements it was very possible that Nicholas was in for a disappointment, but I had no choice but to forge on with my plan. I had presented the danger to the al-Nasir in terms of provoking another Crusade, but I was more concerned with saving two thousand lives.

If there is one quality that unites all tyrants, it is a craving for legitimacy. "I will meet with the Caliph," he said at once. "But it will be to discuss the terms of his surrender."

He was so enthusiastic that I was afraid he might

demand to see al-Nasir on his own, and my plan depended on him bringing his lieutenants along with him. "As you wish," I said quickly, "and which of your men will accompany you?"

He paused to consider my question, and then selected three boys from inside the tent to go with us. I had horses waiting for us, and after Nicholas had given me the requisite warning not to betray him, we made for the city.

This time we passed through the gates of Jaffa, and if the sheer bulk of the thirty foot walls at all impressed the child general he failed to show any outwards signs of it. I supposed that, to a soldier of God, these walls must not pose any more obstacle than the Mediterranean. The Lord would provide.

His lieutenants, however, were another story. Their names were Steg, Andre, and Russ, and each of them came from some different backwater of Europe. Their common language was broken German, perhaps picked up from other boys in their travels. It was readily apparent that none of them had ever seen a city of any size. Their necks craned at the site of even ordinary wonders, like the size of a diamond cutter's house, or the coloured signs that implored passers-by to try the latest vintage at a local winery.

Nicholas stopped in front of an ancient mud and plaster building with two slitted crosses for windows and a steepled tower. He looked at the structure in confusion and then stepped aside as two dark-skinned men entered.

"What is this building used for?" he asked me.

"Surely you've seen a church before, Nicholas."

"I have," he said quickly. "But never a Moslem church."

"They are called mosques. And you have yet to see one. This is a Christian church. We can go in and pray if you'd like?"

Nicholas stepped back into the street, as if to get a better view. Then he shook his head and turned away from it. "No thank you."

He was silent for the rest of our journey through the city.

Our meeting with the Caliph was to take place in his private gardens. Dozens of gardeners had sculpted hedges into the shapes of creatures he'd killed during his reign—the Lion of Cairo, a wild boar from Hungary, a river monster that was said to have attacked him in Persia. A large table had been set in the middle of the lawn, and it had been laden down with pastries, jellies, and all manner of fruit juices, but al-Nasir himself was nowhere to be found.

Steg, Russ, and Andre snatched pastries off the table before they'd even climbed into their seats and stuffed them into their mouths. I wondered how long it had been since they'd had a decent meal and cautioned them to eat slowly.

Nicholas lingered. He appeared to have shaken the mood he'd acquired outside the church. "Where is the Caliph?"

"He asked that you be allowed to eat your fill before he meets with you. It is bad luck in the Holy Land to negotiate on an empty stomach." There was no such superstition of course, but I was desperate and the ruse seemed to work. The general joined his lieutenants at the table.

I paced, hoping to catch sight of one of the Caliph's servants who might tell me what had become of al-Nasir. He was too smart to risk upsetting Nicholas, wasn't he? My plan had been to show the boy general the Caliph's good side and then take him and his lieutenants up in a hot air balloon that would allow them to see the full might of the Caliph's armies. The carrot and then the stick, so to speak. Without the carrot, I worried how Nicholas of Cologne would react to the stick.

"Tell the Caliph that he can come out now. We're full," said the general, suppressing a belch. His breeches were streaked with jam where he'd used them to wipe his fingers.

I couldn't think up another excuse to explain al-Nasir's absence. "Just a moment," I said desperately as I scanned the gardens nearby. Perhaps the Caliph might still arrive?

Nicholas sat for a moment longer and then called out to his lieutenants. "We're leaving."

"Just wait. Please," I begged. "I'm certain that he will be along presently."

"You told us he wanted to speak with us as equals. Is this how you treat an equal?" he asked.

I was already angry with him for crucifying the boys I'd shown the *camera obscura*, and for the fact that his delusions were putting thousands of lives in danger, but it was the look of smug satisfaction on his face that finally broke me.

"He has an *empire* to run," I said caustically. "Did you honestly believe that a man who has faced thousands of Egyptian chariots in battle, who has led tens of thousands into battle and faced death alongside them would be scared of a couple of thousand boys at his doorstep?"

Nicholas remained silent and that infuriated me further.

"What did you think you were going to do? Honestly? Ask God to blow the gates of Jaffa off their hinges and then strike down its garrison of ten thousand heavily armed soldiers? You're an idiot. It's only because the Caliph wanted to avoid slaughtering every single one of you that you've been allowed to go on this long."

Though I'd loomed over him in my anger, he didn't take a single solitary step back. "God will provide," he said simply.

"That's not how God works!" I snapped back.

A long moment of silence stretched out between us. Steg, Russ, and Andre stood nearby. I wondered how much they'd understood with their broken German.

At last, Nicholas seemed to take the high road, which made me hate him all the more. "We'll rejoin our army now. On the morrow we'll see what kind of miracles God has wrought, and for whom."

The journey back through the city was akin to a funeral procession, though I'm certain we all mourned different cadavers. Without the Caliph's help, I was certain that these boys would die and an invasion from Europe would soon follow, resulting in many more deaths. Worse, I wondered if my tirade had helped things along that path. Would I bear some of the responsibility for what was to come?

A commotion at the front gate brought me out of my foul mood. Great billows of smoke rose from just outside the city walls and I could hear many high-pitched screams.

"My men!" yelled Nicholas, wild-eyed. He and his lieutenants dashed off, swords and daggers drawn and I went with them. I never occurred to me that only moments from now, I might be fighting against them for my very life.

Dozens of wagons crowded the gates and I began

to smell burning meat. Our group passed through the open gate and drew up short. A line of charcoal several hundred feet long had been laid out in front of the Child Army and lit on fire. Dozens of spits turned above the glowing coals. Children with greasy fingers and glistening faces ate barely cooked meat with their bare hands and shouted for more. To their credit, some of the older boys had ordered their charges into lines, especially around the dessert table, which held candied dates and figs, as well as lumps of chewy candy from the East that had been dusted with icing sugar.

"My army," said Nicholas with a mixture of awe and disappointment.

Russ, Andre, and Steg whooped and ran off to join the line, ignoring their general's pleas to remain. They had just eaten lunch, but boys of a certain age are known to have two stomachs and these were no different.

I was as stunned as Nicholas. Some of the children who'd finished eating were chasing each other in an impromptu game of tag.

"What trickery is this?" the child general demanded of me. "You've stolen my army from me!"

He launched himself at me before I could answer his charge. I barely got my hands up in time to fend off his dagger. Though he could not have been more than half my weight, my heel caught on the uneven terrain and I fell backwards.

I saw a flash of brown hair and then steel again and flung my gauntlet out. He was on my chest and the weight of my armour made it hard to throw him off. I felt something sharp press against the mail near my ribs and then withdraw. Had I been unarmoured the blow would surely have been lethal.

I rolled over quickly, but he leapt off me and then leapt back on before I could get back to my feet. This time the dagger sank into my shoulder and caught in my collarbone. Pain darkened my vision and I struggled to stay conscious. My father had been a warrior even if I wasn't one, I told myself. Surely I could withstand a little pain.

Nicholas yanked the dagger free and my vision twisted again as blood spurted out of the wound and splattered down my amour. Instinctively, I pressed my hand to the wound, and it was this action, I was later informed by the Caliph's chirurgeons, that had probably saved my life.

Half-blind with pain, I raised my mailed fist and swung it around in a ferocious backhand that, if it had landed, would surely have knocked the boy senseless. But I stopped its swing at the last moment and held my curled fist where it was, mere inches from his face. He'd flinched away from the blow and I waited for him to open his eyes before I spoke.

"A Saracen Caliph has shown you charity today and I would be a poor knight indeed if I did not do the same. Go away. Go away, and never return."

I turned my back on him, half expecting a knife in the back, but it never came. When I turned back around, he was gone. Melted into the crowd of boys. The day's final miracle.

We found him several weeks later—after we'd located homes or apprenticeships, or even places in the regular army for most of the boys in the Child Army— in the very same church he'd refused to enter on the way to his meeting with the Caliph.

It's possible that he believed he could use his powers of oration to sow religious dissent from inside the city walls, or perhaps he just liked to preach. Either way, the priest who ran the church was happy to have him, despite having to put up with some overly enthusiastic sermons.

I still check in with some of the children, now grown into men. One is a successful baker. Another, a potter. Steg is a commander in the Caliph's army, and he writes occasionally to confess his fears that he might soon have to fight his former countrymen in Egypt.

Though there will be some among you who will refuse to believe that a Saracen Caliph saved the lives of two thousand Christian children, you need only note the pale faces that grace the streets of Jaffa to know that it is so. Thus, I implore you to rethink this foolish Crusade you are about to launch in the Holy Land. Let God's country remain the land of peace that it has become, and I assure you that it will persist for all time.

Yours,
Sir Robert Nevsky of Laufenthal.

***

IN ACTUAL HISTORY

The real Children's Crusade had a much more tragic ending than what is written here. Nicholas of Cologne never made it out of Europe. Instead, he gathered about 30,000 children and tried to march them over the Alps to Italy, promising that the sea would dry up before them and they could march on to the Holy Land. Most of those who followed him died on the voyage. When word returned to his village of the disaster, parents and families of those who'd died were so upset, they arrested and later hanged his father. When the survivors finally arrived in Genoa and the promised miracles failed to occur, many of Nicholas' remaining followers abandoned him. Although the Pontiff was said to have treated him kindly upon his arrival in the Papal States, he was unable to muster much support for a Crusade and wandered around Italy for a time before attempting a return to Rhineland. He died as many of his followers had, of hunger and exposure in the Alps' mountain passes.

ABOUT JORDAN ELLINGER

Jordan Ellinger has been called a "standout" in a starred review in Publishers Weekly. He is a member of the Science Fiction and Fantasy Writers Association (SFWA), is a first place winner of Writers of the Future, a graduate of the prestigious Clarion West writers workshop, an award-winning screenplay writer, and author of more than twenty works of fiction, including popular series and media tie-ins (i.e. *Warhammer* and *Star Citizen*). He has collaborated with internationally best-selling authors like Mike Resnick and Steven Savile (with whom he co-authored *Martyrs*, a military thriller). He is also a game designer. His most recent game, *Dragon Assault*, has just been released on Facebook.

MASS

By Luke Bean

The Cazenave Market at 114 Ruda d'Orange was one of the last supermarkets in downtown Marselha, but then the manager disappeared at the end of March. Nobody was sure whether M. Martin had emigrated to Canada or killed himself. Abelia Esperta was his assistant manager, and he hadn't even told her. She simply showed up at the market one day and found her last two coworkers milling around outside a locked door.

"Martin's dead," Ramon argued, "My aunt went to the same meeting hall as him, and he invited her to his consolamentum. He's obviously dead."

"Just because he's a perfect doesn't mean he's *dead*," Abelia snapped, less because she thought he was wrong and more because she felt compelled to dispute anything Ramon declared obvious. She tried to calm her voice. "Is the company going to send anyone else?"

Ramon and Isabel stared at her. "We thought you might know," Ramon said. So Abelia looked up Cazenave Markets on her phone and tried to figure out what number to call while Ramon jiggled his knee and Isabel picked at her dry lips. She called the human resources department, and then the customer service line, and then the press contact line, but none of them picked up. Eventually Ramon suggested they elect an acting manager, Abelia won with two-thirds of the vote (Ramon voted for himself), and she began the hike back to her apartment to pick up the spare set of keys.

The streets were empty. Years of high emigration, mass consolamenta, and the one-child law made sure of that. Abelia had liked when they were busy. Forcing her way through a crowd made her feel like she had mass and momentum. These days, navigating the wilting city felt like she'd shown up to a dream after the dreamer woke up. Every person she saw in public took on greater significance. Strangers would cross the street to talk to her, touching her on the shoulder or elbow to prove they existed.

Even the homeless were mostly gone. Those who hadn't taken consolation had decamped for the Catholic Quarter. The Quarter still thrived, a fungal growth of normalcy on the corpse of Marselha. It crept beyond its old walls further each day as Catholics raised the crucifix above old Cathar meeting halls and raced to claim abandoned apartments before German colonists. One time a group of Catholic boys had followed Abelia home, first corralling her into small talk, then moving on to crude remarks and kissing noises. She'd forced the apartment door shut on them, and they'd spent the next ten minutes hissing lewd nothings through the mail slot. The oldest of them couldn't have been more than fourteen. Abelia had avoided the Catholic Quarter since then. Her close-cropped hair marked her as a Cathar, and it was not a fit place for a Cathar to be.

***

The apartment door was propped open by a chair. Abelia climbed over the chair and found her elderly neighbor, M. Boschona, lingering in the lobby.

"Ought to keep this sort of thing in the meeting hall," he grumbled, gesticulating towards the stairs. "At very least go outside. No decency."

Abelia almost asked what happened, but found her voice rusty from disuse. As she climbed the stairs she noticed trickles of blood dripping from the floors above. Abelia wrinkled her nose and forged ahead, sticking to the wall to avoid getting blood on her shoes. She found the corpse folded backwards around a metal railing on the third floor. Male, chubby, middle-aged, could be anyone. She grabbed his hair and tilted his face up to confirm it was nobody she knew, then let him slump back onto the railing.

"Have you called Removals?" she shouted down to Boschona.

"They should have been here half an hour ago," he called back.

Abelia took a few steps back and made a running hop over the puddle of gore on the landing. When she reached her apartment, she sunk into her desk chair and spun idly for a few minutes. It'd be easy to let inertia take over. Don't bother with the keys, forget about the market, no need to climb over splattered neighbors, just keep spinning until everything outside goes away.

But she had a sudden vision of Ramon running the market, arguing with customers over expired coupons and smirking at Isabel's accent. She shuddered at the thought. She fished the spare keys out of a drawer and headed downstairs. Boschona had taken a seat on the end of the stairs and was sputtering vague invectives under his breath.

It didn't seem right to leave the old man fuming here, waiting for a Removals team that might well take hours. Abelia tapped him on the shoulder. "Would you like to come wait with me at the market? Forget Removals, they can fill out the paperwork themselves."

Boschona clapped his hands together with such force that it made Abelia flinch. "Ah! Yes. Very kind of you. You've always been kind to me." Abelia struggled to think of a time she had shown him any kindness other than brief pleasantries. Then again, Boschona's husband had died recently, so it was possible that any interaction counted as a kindness in his books. They set off together, Boschona steadying himself on Abelia's arm. She could not remember when she had last walked side by side with anyone.

***

Abelia spent the morning of her first day as acting manager in M. Martin's office—well, *her* office—squinting at documents, trying to figure out which papers she filled out to record paychecks and which phone numbers would make trucks arrive with more groceries.

Martin's records showed that the market was hemorrhaging money. This was not a surprise; it was a good day if the market saw even twenty customers. They were losing a fortune in franchise fees alone. She penned a letter to Cazenave Markets in her very best French, politely announcing that the store at 114 Ruda d'Orange was declaring its independence. She had no expectation that anyone would ever read or act on it.

Abelia emerged from the office around lunchtime. She was surprised to find that not only was Boschona still here, he was attracting company. Ramon and a customer had pulled over stools to where Boschona was sitting. The customer had bought a couple of bottles of wine and a bag of chips, which they were passing around the circle, choking with laughter all the while. "Tell Esperta what you told me!" demanded Ramon.

Boschona wheeled on Abelia, red-faced and roaring. "You know why President Normandeau gives speeches behind that big podium? So you can't see the Kaiser crouched down there with his hand up our President's ass. Throw every fucking colonist in the sea, I say." Boschona segued into a graphic description of what he'd do if he ever found himself alone with the President.

Abelia managed to extricate herself from the monologue, leaving Ramon and the customer hooting and egging Boschona on. She found Isabel watching from afar, idly kicking her legs from her perch on a checkout counter. "How long have they been like this?" she asked.

"They, ah…" Isabel blushed. Her Occitan was somewhat shaky, and the combination of self-consciousness and her naturally nervous disposition could make even basic conversations difficult. "Hm. Two hours?" She smiled, but the accelerated kicking of her legs betrayed her anxiety.

"And he's buying snacks?" Abelia asked. Isabel nodded. "Are you busy?" Isabel waggled her eyebrows sheepishly: *Do I look busy?*

***

157

When she first moved to downtown Marselha, Abelia had attended services at the Friends of Mary Meeting Hall for a few months. As with so much in her life, her faith was largely a product of inertia. Abelia was Cathar because her parents had been Cathar; she had no other reason, but that one was good enough. She'd even kept the piously-gender-neutral haircut. But when the congregants at Friends of Mary whirled and danced and spoke in tongues, Abelia felt more embarrassed than ecstatic. She knew where they kept the chairs, though, and meeting halls didn't have locks.

"Old…" said Isabel, running her hand along the elaborate carvings on the front door. It was true—Friends of Mary had seen three centuries of continuous use until the congregation had taken a mass consolamentum last year. When they stepped inside, it became obvious the hall had been turned over by scavengers. Every door was flung open and scattered prayer books carpeted the floor. Isabel traced the sign of the fish on her chest and mumbled something in Vietnamese. The chairs were still stacked in the closet, though, and Abelia and Isabel were soon ferrying them back to the market four at a time.

"When was the last time you saw people just sitting and talking?" Abelia explained, her voice trembling with excitement. Isabel shook her head. "We've got… a *place*. Or we could have a place. I think people need that now."

She fetched markers, posterboard, and duct tape from the crafts section and dumped them outside. Within a few minutes later, she had modified the sign on the front of the store to read "CAZENAVE MARKET—*AND SALON.*" When they'd pushed aside the crates of bread and circled up the chairs in the bakery, they wound up with nearly thirty empty seats. Abelia took that as a promise.

***

A small knot of locals had soon started hanging out at the market to gossip and listen to Boschona pontificate. Passersby drawn in by the sight of people drinking and chatting would linger at the doorway as if they'd break the illusion by going inside. Men and women reminisced over long-disbanded sports teams and swapped rumors about misbehaving perfecti and laid bets on whether Germany or America would be the first to let the missiles fly. They talked in a frenzy and interrupted each other constantly as if weeks of silence had built up a high-pressure backlog of words. Abelia had a hard time remembering what things had been like before the world started to end, but she liked to imagine it was something like this.

Within two weeks the building was barely recognizable as a supermarket. A book club held meetings in the wine section, women took their morning walks down the frozen foods aisle, and M. Boschona (who was regarded by the market's patrons as first among equals) held court behind the seafood counter. They even had a Catholic, a young man named Faure, who had come to proselytize but now seemed more interested in finding excuses to spend time with Isabel than in saving souls. Boschona gnashed his teeth and demanded Faure's expulsion, but Isabel's Occitan *was* improving from practicing with him, so Abelia let him stay.

**

On Abelia's twenty-fourth day as manager, Mme. Cabrol, who lived in an apartment above the market, offered to donate her wide-screen television and two worn-out couches. This news was greeted with wild excitement from the market's patrons, many of whom now practically lived there. In honor of the event, and to clear out the produce section to make way for their new movie theater, Abelia announced that all fruit would be free for the rest of the day.

Later, looking around at a floor slick with melon pulp and shelves covered in sticky red palm prints and Ramon dribbling raspberry bits out of the corners of his mouth, Abelia reflected that she might have overdone the generosity a little bit. But if everyone else was happy stuffing their faces with fruit, who was she to feel differently? The gravity of the market had pulled them into a single mass, a happy, sticky, strawberry-smeared ball.

Out of nowhere, Isabel threw back her head and howled. She deflected everyone's stares with a possessed grin. "Cantaloupe," she said, hefting the melon in her lap and shaking her head at how obvious it was. "Wolf-song." Ramon rolled his eyes and the others went back to the sticky feast, but Abelia laughed so hard that she choked on a mouthful of strawberries. She tried to get out of her chair but she slipped and fell to her knees, and remained there coughing up strawberry chunks and trying to control her pained giggling. Isabel guided her to the staff bathroom, furiously apologizing the whole way, though she was clearly a bit pleased that she'd made Abelia laugh.

The bathroom didn't have a mirror. Most did these days, but M. Martin had always held to the words of the Argentine: "Mirrors and copulation are abominable, for both increase the number of man." It may have discouraged vanity but it also made it hard for Abelia to clean the strawberry pulp from herself. Isabel had to wipe her off like a toddler.

"Don't squirm," Isabel scolded her.

"Squirm's a good word," Abelia said. "Your Occitan's getting better. Better than the last time I told you that, even."

Isabel flushed with pride. "Don't say that," she protested, "You'll make me think too hard about it."

Abelia shrugged. "You've got a good teacher. A… good-*looking* teacher, wouldn't you say?" She leaned in, reveling in Isabel's growing embarrassment.

"He's Catholic, Bee!" said Isabel, flicking strawberry pulp off of a paper towel back into Abelia's face. Abelia licked it up with all the dignity she could muster. "You're ridiculous," Isabel said sternly. She rested her head on Abelia's shoulder.

They laid back and spent a moment digesting. "I told my perfect about the market," Isabel said. "He wants to come by some time."

"As a guest, or as a perfect?"

"Both."

"Is he planning to offer consolation?"

"Yes."

Abelia licked her fingers and considered this. "Ok," she said.

***

That night, police beat a Catholic teenager to death. The police commissioner said he was wanted for burglary, and had resisted arrest. The Bishop of Marselha said the boy was just another scavenger looking for his next meal, and urged all Marselhans to demand justice for his murder. Riots began in the Catholic Quarter the next day.

***

The vows of the consolamentum, taken to become a perfect, were demanding and immalleable. One act of violence, one taste of meat, one romantic dalliance, and you were damned to reincarnate on this earth for another lifetime of spiritual imprisonment. In the past, most Cathars did not take consolation until they were near death, to avoid a lifetime of temptation. Now many sped up the process by committing suicide. The Perfect Laurent Aubanel had taken his vows at the age of 18, during the height of the Third Revival, and as far as anyone knew he had kept them these last thirty years. He sat with his legs crossed on top of the bakery counter.

"The world mocks our faith as a death cult," said Aubanel. He unfolded a newspaper on his lap. His finger landed on the headline: GERMANY EXPELS US AMBASSADOR. "You show me a nation preparing for war and I'll show you a death cult." He was the quiet sort of perfect, the sort who made you lean in to catch every word. "This article refers to Germany as an ally of France. They are wrong. I know the word for a country who wants your children to die for their ambition: *enemy*."

He paused to fold up the newspaper. He placed it back in his lap, then took a long, searching look around his new congregation before he spoke again. "I've spoken to some of you before. I know some of you have been driven from your homes by persecution. The nations criminalize abortion because they need more flesh to hold more guns. They criminalize 'assisted suicide' so they can lock us away for setting souls free. How many of my friends here chose their faith over their homeland? Stand, if you don't mind." Isabel stood. Nine or ten others. The perfect leaned in to meet his rapt congregation and though he spoke barely above a murmur, his voice came from everywhere. "You, my brave brothers and sisters, you know not to fear the death of the body. It is the death of the soul we fear, and let me tell you this: *a nation is a death cult.* Will the end come with rains of blood?"

No, breathed the crowd.

"Will it come with magical whores riding many-headed beasts?"

No.

"Will Hell open up to drag down the wicked?"

No.

"Hell is *here* and Hell is *now!* When the end comes, it will be at the hands of the nations who clung so tight to this *filthy* existence. And this is the only omen you'll need." He flung the newspaper into the crowd. As the sheets fluttered apart each one cried of military buildups and unbearable provocations.

"We are witnessing the last generation of man," said Aubanel, and his breath was ragged, as if his message was a physical burden. "Everyone here has been offered one last chance at grace, if only you reach out and take it. Do you think we'll see another month pass before the Catholics or the Germans control this country? Another year before the nations bathe the world in fire? Whatever plans God has for us, we're reaching the end of His schedule."

As the men and woman of the Cazenave Market joined hands and prayed, Abelia felt God, or something enough like God that the difference didn't matter to her. The inertia of the crowd swept her along. Boschona, on her right, shouted praise, and Abelia shouted too. Isabel, on her left, started crying, and Abelia cried too. Aubanel asked if they would accept consolation, and they accepted, and Abelia accepted too.

***

The riots continued into their sixth day. They had not yet come down the Ruda d'Orange, but smoke from the fires was visible at all hours. Most patrons of the market had stopped going home, and now slept on mats and blankets scattered around the aisles.

Faure left. He said he needed to make sure his family was safe, but there was a sense that after eight centuries of bloodshed and oppression, there was no longer any room for friendship between Catholic and Cathar. It was asking too much of human nature.

***

Isabel knelt sitting on her ankles. To her left, the newly perfected washed the wax off their hands and then took their place in the audience. To her right sat Abelia and the others waiting their turn. There were only a few left in line. Those who were not ready for perfection had gone home.

The Perfect Laurent Aubanel took one of the prelit candles he'd lined up on the conveyer belt at register 18, and then stood before Isabel. She held out her hands, flat and facing down. She closed her eyes.

He tipped the candle over her left hand, splattering hot wax over her knuckles.

"I reject this pain," she said. Her face did not react.

Ramon held out a scrap of velvet he'd found at a fabric store down the street. Aubanel took it and rubbed it along the back of Isabel's right hand.

"I reject this comfort."

She opened her mouth. Aubanel opened a packet of beef jerky and placed a small piece on her tongue. She kept it balanced on her tongue for five seconds, and then the perfect removed it.

"I will not eat of suffering."

Aubanel picked up a small metal rod that used to be part of a shopping basket. He smacked it across the back of Isabel's left hand, cracking the dried wax.

"I will not raise my hand in anger."

The perfect clasped her right hand with his own. Isabel did not hold his hand, but let hers stiffen.

"I relinquish all love but the love of God and his works."

Aubanel stepped back. Isabel took a deep breath.

"Though I dwell in the Kingdom of Satan, I will strive for the Kingdom of God. I renounce this world and long for the world to come."

Aubanel grasped both her hands, and this time she held his. "Pray with me, my sister."

They bowed their heads and prayed, Aubanel silently and Isabel in Vietnamese. When she finished she stood and stepped to the left.

"Abelia?" Abelia stood.

***

They'd used scented candles for the ceremony. Hours later, a dozen competing scents still clogged the air. You could escape the smell in the back of the store, but everyone was crowded around the windows at the front.

It was hard to see the smoke in the night sky, but every now and then some smoke would blot out a streetlight and Isabel would tense up and bunch closer to Abelia. Ramon fiddled with the spare keys outside in the hope that maybe this time one of them would lower the metal shutter. The rioters hadn't passed down the Ruda d'Orange yet. Maybe it would be a relief when they did. One way or the other, they could go home once the rioters had passed.

"I'm awake," said Boschona from behind Abelia. "You should take my couch. We'll wake you up if anything happens." Abelia made a brief show of protest, but she had only a vague sense of duty keeping her awake and a long day of fretting weighing on her body. It occurred to her that she was being let sleep as a sign of respect. She barely had time to complete the thought before losing consciousness.

***

She was woken by the sound of shouting. She knew they were here, but she wasn't frightened anymore. She was…heightened, or more aware, something else.

She peeked over the couch. Ramon was braced against the door with everyone holding him in place as a small cluster of rioters pushed the door from the other side.

One of the rioters started shouting at the others, and they backed off the door. Three of them together heaved something off the ground, large and dark and heavy, Abelia couldn't tell what it was, but they flung it through the market's display window. The window exploded into a cloud of glass.

Abelia burrowed back under the blanket. Rubber soles squealed as the market patrons rushed for the emergency exit. The looters did not chase them. They moved through the store with silent purpose, filling bags and baskets and retreating back into the night. Within minutes, the looters were gone and the market was still.

Something shattered. She was not alone after all. "We could have sold that, you moron."

Then a reply. "What, you were going to walk home balancing it on your head? 'Yes, officer, I was out taking my television hat for a walk.' Fuck off." She peered out from beneath the blanket. Three looters lingered in her store. One, with wide green eyes and a bandana over his nose and mouth, had just flung something through Mme. Cabrol's television. He was being scolded by another, whose curly blond hair spilled out from underneath a dark baseball cap.

A third stepped between them. "Forget it. There's other stuff." This one had a German accent. A colonist, sent to make sure that when France died Germany had dibs on the corpse. Even the Catholics typically hated colonists, but apparently these boys had set aside the prejudices of their parents.

Abelia boiled. They were stealing from her store. They had driven away her people. They were defiling her place. Cazenave Market was a bubble, and if the world was allowed to poke it, it would pop. As the looters moved past the butcher's counter, towing half-full shopping carts behind them, Abelia crawled out from beneath the blankets and moved to the television. She picked up the can of soup lodged in the center of the screen.

The looters stopped at the pharmacy. Abelia doubled back around the store and approached them through the frozen foods aisle. She leaned around a corner and flung the can at the one with curly hair. She darted back down the aisle without waiting to see where it hit. She heard a yelp of pain. "Someone's here," one of them said—the one with wide eyes, judging by the voice. "Find something heavy and stick together." She scampered three aisles down, then listened as the looters methodically snaked their way towards her.

You don't have to win. You just have to be more trouble than you're worth. That was how the early Cathars had survived through the Crusades and the Inquisition and the Wars of Religion and a thousand trials more. Pretend to convert, run when you can, fight when you must— inertia is on your side. Catharism had dominated France for four hundred years, yet here Abelia was, trapped in a historical reenactment.

She could hear soft breathing on the other side of the shelf. She mapped out aisle five in her mind. They walked past the Catalan food…pasta…tomato sauce…*tomato sauce.*

Abelia lowered her shoulder and charged the shelf. Boxes of Special K burst under her weight, filling the air with cereal dust. The shelf rocked forward, showering glass and tin and tomato onto the looters. She paused to hear the howls of pain (and howls of laughter from one of them, apparently unharmed). Her muscles tensed to run, but she realized that the looters weren't moving, just standing on the other side of the aisle whispering. Debating whether to leave?

"On three," one of them whispered, and the shelf shivered faintly as six hands braced against it, and before Abelia's mind had a chance to process what was happening her legs knew it was time to move. *Every action has an equal and opposite reaction.*

She pushed off with her left foot. Her right foot landed on a box of Special K. *A good assistant manager ensures the aisles are clean and accessible at all times.* "One."

Her legs vanished from under her, swept aside in a puff of cereal, and she fell to the ground. The linoleum was cool and gritty and so, so unbearably solid. *Did you know the Kellogg brothers were Cathars?* her brain informed her stupidly. "Two."

Abelia brushed off the pain and cereal and forced herself to run. She had never appreciated just how long aisle four was. Everything depended on whether they pushed on "One, two, THREE" or on "One, two, three, PUSH." That extra fraction of a second would be enough to make it out of the aisle. "Three."

They pushed on three. *Aisle four. Coffee, tea, biscuits, assorted breakfast food.*

Abelia did not see aisle four fall; it was simply upright one moment and on top of her the next. Her face was again pressed into the linoleum. Everything below her chest was trapped under three hundred pounds of coffee, tea, biscuits, assorted breakfast foods, and the shelf on which they belonged. Soon, she knew, this would hurt tremendously. She tried to look back to see if the other shelves had toppled like dominoes— she had sometimes wondered if they could—but found she could not turn her head more than a couple degrees. She could barely wiggle her legs, never mind work them free. *An object at rest remains at rest unless acted on by an outside force.*

The store was lost. It didn't matter if they cleaned up. It would be like trying to blow air into a popped balloon. All she could hope was that the looters would take what they wanted and leave her alone.

No such luck. The one with wide eyes kneeled in front of her, laying his head so close to hers that his breath warmed her face. "Hi," he said, removing his bandana. His smile might have seemed disarming if not for the trickles of blood and fragments of glass covering his face. "We've decided to forgive you for…" He motioned to his wounds as he trailed off. "We got off on the wrong foot. We just want to help you." The one with curly hair and the German knelt next to him, holding a box of saltines and a bottle of grape juice. "Starting with your first mass."

"My name is Abelia Esperta," she managed to gasp. The shelf weighed heavy on her lungs. She only had one breath in which to humanize herself. "I grew up in La Rochèla. I studied physics at Aix-Marselha Univ—" The end of her sentence was drowned out with bitter laughter. She had accidentally struck a nerve. "You aren't one of us just yet, then," Wide Eyes said with forced mirth. "What lazy, criminal Catholic would be allowed a spot at Aix-Marselha University?" He wedged two fingers between Abelia's lips and forced a saltine into Abelia's mouth.

"What business would employ a wicked Catholic when they could hire a righteous Cathar?" Another saltine. This one scratched her gums. She could taste blood flavoring the crackers.

"What responsible Cathar father would let his daughter consort with the ancient enemy?" Wide Eyes glanced at Curly Hair, whose face contorted with emotion. A reference to a painful memory, no doubt. Wide

Eyes held Abelia's head back while Curly Hair tipped grape juice into her mouth. She coughed juice onto the floor and gasped for air.

"Don't you want to know what it's like?" He reached into his jacket and pulled out a long glass shard, salvaged from a broken jar of tomato sauce. He ran his thumb back and forth along the shard, making a faint squeaking sound. "So many years of pain, and so little time to convey it…" *Bite his hand if he gets close. Make him drop the glass. They don't know you have your arms free, but your legs, what to do about your legs…*

Curly Hair grabbed his arm. "We already taught her a lesson. Let's go." Wide Eyes just grinned and wriggled free.

"Do you think I'm overreacting, Abelia Esperta?" he said, meeting her gaze. His soft green eyes grew bigger and bigger and his thumb squeaked on the glass over and over. He turned to the German. "Do you think I'm overreacting, Paul?"

The German glanced back and forth between his friends as if hoping one would tell him what he thought. "Yes," he finally mumbled. "Too far."

"Well," said Wide Eyes. His shard of glass lazily drifted toward his friends. "Well, well."

Curly Hair took a step back. "Don't you do anything stupid, okay?" Wide Eyes shook his head with a disingenuous grin. Curly Hair clenched and unclenched his hands. A few of his curls clung to a sweaty brow. "We're going to get the police. Don't you touch her, okay? Tell me you won't." Wide Eyes nodded, the very picture of obedience. Curly Hair and the German fled the market. And Abelia was alone with Wide Eyes.

Wide Eyes turned back to Abelia. "Don't worry

about them." Behind him, the staff door opened quietly. She had left it locked. *If someone can distract him long enough for me to get my legs free*—and there was Isabel, it was really her, and she was shuffling through the wine section, and Wide Eyes was squeaking his thumb on the glass again, and Isabel was picking up a bottle of cheap pinot noir, and she could feel Wide Eyes' breath on her face, and Isabel was standing behind him—*no, Isabel, think of your soul*—and Abelia's eyes gave her away. Wide Eyes followed her line of sight, and wheeled around, glass at the ready, but it was too late. Isabel brought the bottle crashing down into his face with all her strength.

She jumped back and scuttled to a safe distance. Wide Eyes' left eye was red and swollen like a plum, the bloody lump in the center of his face barely recognizable as something that had recently been a nose. He lay on his back, his feet scrabbling to regain control of the ground and the hand with the glass shard in it lifted in an empty threat. Isabel crept forward again, and stomped on the hand holding the glass over and over until glass and hand were united.

And there were Ramon and Aubanel, and they were lifting the shelf off of Abelia, and Isabel was dragging her out by her shoulders, and Boschona was taping Wide Eyes' hands behind his back. Isabel was crying. For a moment Abelia thought Isabel was crying for her. Then she realized Isabel was crying for herself.

"I would have let you die," Isabel said bitterly. "But you broke your vows. I saw you. I could have let you die otherwise."

Abelia nodded. She slumped on Isabel's shoulder and let herself be carried out into the smoky night. The last thing she remembered from that night was Aubanel on the phone with Removals, asking if they could make a morning pickup. She was sorry to have dragged Isabel down with her. But she was glad to be alive.

***

IN ACTUAL HISTORY

In 1209, Pope Innocent III declared a crusade against the Cathar heretics in southern France. Catharism was an unusual sect of Christianity, sometimes described as "Christian Buddhism." The Cathars believed that the material world had been created by Satan, and souls were trapped in human bodies, doomed to reincarnate until they were freed by the rejection of the material world. Catharism encouraged pacifism, vegetarianism, and gender equality, and opposed capital punishment, marriage, and procreation.

Though the local nobility was Catholic, they bore no ill will towards their Cathar subjects. They perceived the Albigensian Crusade for what it was: a ploy by the King of France to subjugate the independent southern lords. Many Catholic lords, most notably Count Raymond VI of Toulouse and King Peter II of Aragon, rallied in opposition to the French crusaders. They were defeated, and Catharism was annihilated in a wave of forced conversions and massacres. The brutality of the Albigensian Crusade is immortalized in the instructions given to French forces preparing to sack the Cathar stronghold of Béziers: "Kill them all. God will know his own."

In the world of Mass, the Albigensian Crusade has been defeated, Catharism has become the dominant religion of France, and Catholics are a downtrodden minority. The Occitan language and culture of southern France has flourished rather than fading away—the city known in the story as Marselha is known to us as Marseilles. Though the terms "Cathar" and "Perfect" were invented by their enemies, the Cathars have adopted the terms as their own.

One lingering question surrounds the Cathars: did they really encourage ritual suicide to avoid temptation after taking the consolamentum? Though the practice was reported, it may have been fabricated as anti-Cathar propaganda, since the consolamentum was typically performed on those who were on their deathbed anyway. Whether medieval Cathars practiced ritual suicide or not, religions change over time, and the denomination featured in Mass certainly does.

ABOUT LUKE BEAN

Luke Bean is a recent graduate from New York University, where he studied film and history. His story "Company" appeared in *What If? The Anthology of Alternate History*. He lives in New York, where he spends his days tutoring history students and his nights crouched in his apartment, building up his portfolio of screenplays.

THE BORDER MEN

By Axel Kylander

"A ruler must always take the most honorable of actions. If a ruler chooses to compromise his honor, he slays his soul and that of his realm."

-Bleddyn ap Cynfyn of House Mathrafal, The First of His Name, by the Grace of God, King of the Britons, author of *Speculum ob Principes*, 1070 Anno Domini.

1366 Anno Domini

Roman Exarchate of Poland

The fire appeared suddenly, flaring up in the distance. Faint fingers of lights reached through the trees, brushing against six men on sturdy rounceys. The night had been moonless, black as pitch, so dark a man could scarcely see his hand in front of his face. Bleddyn ap Maredudd of House Mathrafal felt naked and vulnerable.

Silently, unanimously, the six of them dismounted, travel-worn boots crunching softly on needles and cones. Bleddyn's horse whickered, too loudly, and he laid a soothing hand on her neck. The others were already prepared. *Waiting for me.* He could feel their eyes watching him. With nervous fingers made clumsy by gloves and the cold, he fumbled with straps, trying to keep the metal buckles from clanking. He slung his quiver across his chest, and tied his rouncey to a tree, the beast stamping her hooved feet, as though to protest being left behind. Bleddyn strung his longbow, giving it a gentle pull to make sure it was tight. His comrades stood silent as gargoyles, but he could feel their impatience. He nodded, and they began to move, the darkness concealing the flush of embarrassment creeping up his neck.

They crouched low, creeping through the forest with swift, quiet feet. Bleddyn weaved through the close-grown pines, cursing softly as twigs snapped beneath his boots. There was a slight ridge up ahead. Beyond that, the others had told him, the forest came to an abrupt end, and a small village sat on flat ground just beyond. Bleddyn's heart raced, but he had grown so cold he almost welcomed the thought of a fire whatever the circumstances. Their boots dug into the soft forest floor as they reached the top of the gently-sloped ridge.

***

The entire village was ablaze, the thatched roofs of huts sending up great billows of black smoke as the orange flames licked higher. The air was filled with the cries of innocents. They ran back and forth as their attackers rode or shot them down. The raiders on foot were searching the burning buildings for loot. A new shriek filled the air as a man emerged from the nearest hut, dragging a woman by her hair. He threw down his spear and forced himself on top of her, tearing her dress open down the middle. His companions laughed with guttural voices. *It's true then. They are savages.*

"Nock." Sir Jacques said suddenly, his raspy voice quiet and emotionless. Bleddyn reached over his right shoulder, took an arrow between two fingers, and set it on the bowstring. His heart was climbing up his throat, throbbing with uneven pulses. "Draw." The order came, and Bleddyn pulled the string back, his bow arcing heavily as he targeted the shadowy rapist. "Loose."

Time seemed to slow as the bowstring twanged and the arrow thrummed through the air. Bleddyn watched numbly as the sharp metal head buried itself in the man's neck several yards away. His companions were already drawing again, and Bleddyn remained still, watching the black liquid flow from the shadow's neck.

The other savages had noticed something was amiss, possibly because they had lost at least eight of their number. They charged, on foot and on horses, across the burning village to the tree line. Bleddyn came to his senses, and managed to draw again as the attackers closed in. He loosed, and the arrow sang its war-song as it flew into the eye of a raider. The man bent over backwards in his saddle before falling to the frozen dirt.

Bleddyn dropped his bow and drew his sword. As he ran forward, an arrow shaft dug into the throat of a horse, sending its rider rolling away. *What am I doing?* His feet were moving of their own accord. He knelt quickly next to the woman who had been raped. She was sobbing uncontrollably, and the firelight revealed the glistening of the blood thick on her thighs. She feebly tried to push him away, stammering something in Polish. He knew Polish, but he wasn't paying attention. *I'm not trying to fuck you!* He wanted to scream, but he seemed to have swallowed his tongue during his mad dash.

He left his sword on the ground, half-carrying, half-dragging the woman away. He set her behind a bush, and saw her face in the firelight. *God, she's no older than me.* "Stay here." He managed to choke out, but he couldn't tell if she understood. The air was alive with the clash of steel-on-steel as he scooped up his sword again. He looked around and saw his companions, engaged with the savage raiders.

***

"Romyn!" A voice he didn't recognize growled. Bleddyn looked back to the tree line. The unhorsed raider was surging forward, his curved sword looking wickedly sharp. He kept shouting.

Bleddyn didn't speak the tongue, but he understood what the man was saying. Suddenly his undergarments were wet, and he could feel the warm piss running down his right leg. The raider raised his sword over his head with two hands as he approached. Bleddyn dodged the brutal downward swing, but only at the last second. The enemy wheeled around, both their footing reversed, Bleddyn held his sword out with both hands, the point wavering as tremors coursed along his arms. The raider laughed throatily, knocking his young enemy's sword aside with the flat of his blade.

Bleddyn stumbled backwards, bringing his weapon over his head in a high guard. The raider thrust quickly, but somehow his blade was blocked, and Bleddyn was dodging to the side. Without thinking, he slammed the sharp length of his sword into the man's belly. He could feel it cutting deep, through skin and flesh and organs, until he heard the *thunk* as it hit his foe's spine. He could feel tears of horror blurring his eyes as he tore the steel free from the man, who was gurgling as he died. The blade gleamed scarlet in the fire light. A river of blood rushed out of the raider as he fell, spraying across Bleddyn's armor. He retched suddenly, vomit spattering onto his boots.

***

"Was this your first?" Konrad nudged the rapist's corpse with a broad boot. Blood had spilled over the dead man's stubbly beard, looking black as the world was filled with the faint blue light of early morning. He was not much older than Bleddyn.

"Yes." Bleddyn said dully. He felt numb, horrified by battle and ashamed he had soiled himself. *At least these dark breeches hide the stain.*

"You'll be wanting a woman then." Konrad continued. He was older by twenty years, plump of stomach and broad of shoulder. He had fled the Exarchate of Germania after bedding the Exarch's youngest daughter. The Exarch cried rape, Konrad insisted it was the girl who started it. But he didn't wait around for judgment, instead fleeing to the forests of Poland, living out his days as a Border Man. Bleddyn didn't know how much of his story was true, or even if Konrad was his real name. "Every man needs a woman after his first fight." He looked at the younger man's pale face. "You look like you need two."

Bleddyn shook his head. "I have a wife, and I'll not dishonor her." *Granted, I barely know her, but vows are vows, and Angharad is the best any man could hope for.* His father made the arrangements, even having his son's wife educated at the Imperial court. She had grown into an extremely talented young woman, as beautiful as she was intelligent, with many admirable traits to her character.

"You should show more respect, Konrad." Sir Jacques approached, wiping off his sword with a tattered rag. His brown eyes fixed on Bleddyn's grey ones, piercing through them as the arrow had pierced the raider's eye. "You fought well, my Prince. Are you injured?"

Only my pride. "No. And you?"

The aging Italian knight shook his head. "I am well, as are the others."

"Where are they?"

"One of the Mongols was wounded. We're interrogating back there. Follow me." Jacques walked back towards one of the ruined huts.

***

Oh, God. Clearly, things were going to get unpleasant. Sir Richard held a long, forward-curving knife across the Mongol's throat, his other hand pulling the captive's head back by the hair. Sir Juan held the man's left forearm, ready to start slicing off fingers with his dagger. An arrow was sticking out of the raider's right shoulder, and his breathing was quick and shallow.

Khudayar the Arab stood over their captive, his

long, willowy shadow falling across the man's face. In a calm voice, he began to speak in the Mongol's strange tongue. Bleddyn turned to Sir Jacques. "What's he saying?"

The old knight's eye never left the interrogation. "Who sent you? Which lord? Are there more raiding parties like yours?"

The Mongol, to his credit, remained resolutely silent. *He's not much older than me either.* He was slightly less silent when Sir Juan's dagger sliced across in a smooth motion, taking his smallest finger. The captive whimpered, but did not cry out. Bleddyn's stomach roiled with disgust. *There is no justice in this. There is no honor in this.* "Stop!"

All eyes fell on him. "Stop." Bleddyn repeated.

"My Prince—" Khudayar began.

The younger man seized the opening. "That's right. I *am* your *Prince.* I am Bleddyn of House Mathrafal. Someday I shall be Emperor of Rome. And in the name of God, I command you to stop this unchristian torture."

Sir Jacques laid a hand on his shoulder. "My Prince, I understand your qualms. You're an honorable man. But we are at war. Not inside the Empire, of course, but it rages on here at the borders, as it has for decades. That is why there are Border Men. Your father sent you to us so you could learn our war, as he learned it in the Arabian territories. If you ride with us, you fight our war. Honor has no place here."

Bleddyn opened his mouth. Nothing came out. He closed it again, and nodded sullenly. The interrogation continued.

Khudayar repeated his questions to the Mongol. He remained silent, and lost another finger for it, blood flowing in rivulets over his maimed hand as tears ran down his cheeks. Sir Richard, overcome by impatience, grabbed the arrow shaft in the prisoner's shoulder and twisted it further into his flesh. The Mongol screamed, and a foul stench filled the air as he lost control of his bowels. He kept saying the same words, over and over again.

"Sirs," the Prince scarcely tried to conceal his contempt, unable to keep the words in his head, "You are men without honor." He left them there, walking with long, swift strides.

"He says he will speak, my Prince." Khudayar called after him. Bleddyn sighed, and turned around.

The prisoner grimaced bitterly as the Prince stood over him, but looked him in the eye. The words were incomprehensible to Bleddyn. All he caught was *Rom*. But the man spoke strongly, shouting his last words, fierce pride on his face. The Border Men's frowns grew deeper and deeper.

Jacques nodded, and Sir Richard slid his broad knife across the Mongol's throat. Blood spurted out in a wide arc from the man's neck, drops of red speckling Bleddyn's face. The dead man went still, the defiant light leaving his eyes.

"What did he say?" The Prince's voice felt hoarse.

"He said..." Sir Jacques was so pale he looked ghostly, "He said they are coming. Hundreds, thousands, and more. They shall cross the borders here, and conquer everything. He said they will burn our churches and loot our castles. They will enslave our children and rape our women. Then they shall take our lives."

***

"I…" Bleddyn found it difficult to speak, "My father educated me himself…he told me the Empire had long ago laid out plans in case the Mongols ever attacked—plans for all the borders."

"You know where we must go, then?" Jacques looked even more grim than usual.

The Prince swallowed nervously. "We must cross the Vistula."

The Vistula was the largest river in the Exarchate of Poland. After more than a century of quietly observing the Mongol conquests, the Empire knew it was important to use terrain against their masses of horse archers. If the Mongols had to cross a river to attack in force, much of their advantage would be lost. They could burn half the Exarchate, but they would need to cross the Vistula to burn the Empire. *Father always said he thought the hammer would fall on Poland.*

Richard and Juan cleaned their blades and slid them into sheathes. "I suppose the legions will already be assembling, then." Juan said, shattering the awkward silence.

Richard nodded. "Aye. The Emperor will have heard of this months ago. I'm sure he has spies in the Khan's court. Plenty of time to assemble the armies in Europe at least. The North African legions might even get there in time, if the weather's good."

"We must be away from here." Sir Jacques's voice cut through Bleddyn's thoughts with a sharp edge of urgency. "The Mongols will take note when this party does not return. The Horde will not be more than a day or two behind us, and there will be other outriders. Gather all the quivers you can find, and perhaps some food."

***

Bleddyn walked past the first man he had killed, a corpse with a now forever young face, blank eyes following him accusingly. He found the woman—*no, girl*—behind the bush where he'd left her. She looked a year or two younger than him, roughly four-and-ten. She was curled in a ball, trembling, staring with eyes as blank as the dead rapist's. Those were wide eyes, and filled with slow-falling tears. Her arms were hugged around her chest, trying to cover budding breasts that had been exposed as the Mongol tore her dress open.

Without thinking, he unfastened his dark green cloak and wrapped it gently around her. The girl flinched when his gloved fingers brushed against her, but clung to the cloak and its warmth all the same.

"You are safe now." He said soothingly in Polish. No response. "I am the Prince of the Empire, my lady. I will allow no harm to befall you." She did not answer. He helped her to her feet, though the girl seemed barely able to stand his touch.

Bleddyn brought her out to the Border Men. "She's the only survivor." The Border Men remained silent. "They raped her." Still nothing. "She needs our help." *It's so obvious. What are they doing?"*

"My Prince," Khudayar's tone was sorrowful but firm, "You have a just heart--an honorable heart--but we have no time for the girl."

Impossible. They're not actually suggesting we... "Leave her?"

"The horses of our foes are long since gone. We have no spare mounts. Even if we did, her injuries would slow us down. The Horde would overtake us. And we are needed."

"Why? Why are we needed? If my father knew months ago that the Mongols were assembling, what does it matter if we die?"

Khudayar did not back down. "You are the heir to the Empire, for one thing. We are sworn to protect you, and we are needed besides. The Emperor must know how close the Horde is, and finish his preparations." The Arab gestured behind him, "These dead men were outriders, My Prince-- hunters and scouts. The Horde is not far. If we leave the girl, we shall hear them soon. If we bring the girl, tonight we will hear their arrows chasing us through the trees, and their swords biting our bones. We leave the girl."

Sir Richard was glaring impatiently. "The bitch's mind is as broken as her cunt." He said. "She won't get far before the Mongols finds her. It'd be kinder to cut her throat and be done with it." His hand drifted to the antler hilt of his knife.

The Prince drew his sword. "One more step, Sir, and you shall rot here with the Mongols."

"*Enough.*" It took Bleddyn a moment to realize Sir Jacques was talking to him. "No man bears steel against another in this company, Bleddyn ap Maredudd. Put up your sword."

Abashed, but still angry, the Prince sheathed his blade. The old man continued. "It is as Khudayar says. We do not have time to save the girl, and it is imperative we get to the Emperor with what we know of enemy movements. You may stay here, help the girl, and keep your honor intact. You will die, and it will have been a waste to the Empire and to yourself. But no man will stop you. However, you will *not* deter us from our task. I do not care who you are, heir to the Empire, bastard son of the Pope, or one of Christ's Saints!

Nothing will stop us. We will protect the Empire, or die trying."

***

The Prince looked from the girl, glassy-eyed and trembling, then to the Border Men, cold and implacable. *Stay.* He screamed at himself. *Stay, or dishonor yourself forever. Stay. Stay. STAY.* He shook his head, running his fingers through brown hair made long and tangled from months of traveling in the wild. *Honor has no place here.* He looked up. The sun was rising properly now.

"Very well." Bleddyn ap Maredudd of House Mathrafal said heavily. "Let us leave this place."

The Border Men looked pleased, even Sir Richard. He glanced at the girl again. "You'll be needing that cloak back, Princeling."

He's right. They were in the middle of a chilly autumn, and the cloak wrapped around the girl's shoulder was oh-so-warm. He would freeze if he did not grab it from her shoulders. "It was a gift." the Prince said. "I will not take it back."

A few minutes later, they were walking back into the woods. Bleddyn bent over and picked up his longbow from where he had dropped it. He looked back. The ruins of the village were shrouded in the mist of early morning. The girl was still there, standing exactly where they had left her. Numb fingers gripped at the cloak, and her dress hung loosely off her body, torn and stained. Her eyes stared into the woods like those of a dead thing, and she seemed to fade into the mist. The Prince turned away. That was the last he saw of her.

***

They rode for hours and hours, the days blending together, moving at a cautious but steady pace. The pine trees loomed overhead, and Bleddyn could feel in them the eyes of his ancestors, silent and judging. *My namesake said a ruler must always have honor. The man who built my family said that. What have I done?*

The original Bleddyn Mathrafal had been King of the Britons three hundred years earlier. He had raised the family out of obscurity, and with the Yngling Anarchy in England, had made his house and his kingdom the dominant power in the British Isles. He was described by all sources as a kind, brave, honorable man, untainted by the intrigues of lesser rulers. The original Bleddyn had also been a learned man, and had set his philosophies to writing in a tome entitled *Speculum ob Principes,* A Mirror for Rulers. Every noble boy, including the Prince, studied that great work in their youth. It was Bleddyn's favorite book, and until now, he had lived by its tenets.

A ruler must act with justice, and mercy. Yet he had stood by as the Border Men tortured their captive. *A ruler must use words before swords.* Yet he bared steel against Sir Richard before the words came out. *When matters come to swords, a ruler must be skillful and brave.* Bleddyn did not know where he stood there. He had soiled himself, yes, but he had heard all that men do in their first battle. Besides, he was only six-and-ten, and he had killed three of the enemy. *But what good is a sword without honor?*

He shivered. I should have taken the cloak. The more the chill of the day sank into his bones, the more he knew it to be true. She might be dead already. My cloak lies rotting on the ground, or around some Mongol's shoulders. It had been a waste. The small gift of a cloak did not change the fact that I left her to die.

"Don't they teach Mongolian in the capital?" Sir Juan asked, frowning as his steed trotted next to the younger man's. His was the first voice Bleddyn had heard in hours.

"No." The Prince said. "In Rome, the Mongols are savages, and it's not worth learning how to talk to them. Only how to kill them."

Juan smiled bitterly. "And what do you think now?"

Bleddyn shook his head. "You know, my mother and wet nurse told me stories about them when I was a child and wouldn't go to bed or eat my greens. They said they were demons, coming to carry away little boys that didn't do as they were told."

Juan laughed.

The Prince continued on, the words tumbling out. "But I've fought them now. They are men, and men die. I don't fear them anymore."

"You should." Juan said quietly.

***

They rode day and night, sleeping in the saddle, eating in the saddle, dismounting only to empty their bladders or bowels. Several days into their ride, Bleddyn was lacing up his breeches after pissing against a tree when he heard something. A distant pounding. Quickly, he went back to the Border Men, who were already swinging up into their saddles.

"What's that noise?" He was trying to keep the anxiety out of his voice. In his heart, he knew what it was.

Sir Jacques's hair looked even greyer than usual. To

his horror, Bleddyn saw a flicker of fear in the old man's eyes. "They're getting *closer*," the Border Man said, though whether to himself or Bleddyn, the Prince could not tell.

***

Two days later, they were crossing a broad field of high grass. The footing was treacherous for their mounts, as branches had fallen from the dead trees that stood in the field, waiting to trip an incautious beast. *The ground is rocky, too. Wonderful.* The sun loomed over their heads, but offered no warmth.

"*Look,*" Konrad hissed, nodding behind them. On top of the high hills they had ridden out of were mounted men, dark figures against the pale blue sky. The far off thud of infinitely beating drums that had followed them over the last few days seemed to be growing louder. On the hilltops, the horsemen shouted something.

"Ride!" Jacques shouted from the front of their six-man column.

They rode, fast and hard, dashing across the field of uneven footing. The distant tattoo grew louder and faster, the black figures were surging down the hill. Bleddyn almost bit his tongue off as his rouncey jumped over a fallen tree branch, landing hard on the stony earth. He glanced behind as Juan's steed leapt over the branch. Then came Sir Richard, bringing up the rear guard. His horse was shining with a sweaty lather, and as it jumped over the branch, its back legs caught and it crashed to the ground.

Bleddyn shouted, and the others turned back. "Is your leg broken?" Juan was eyeing the distant Mongols as he spoke.

"No." Richard scowled as he put his steed out of its misery. "What are you standing there for? Keep going!" He notched an arrow to his bow string.

The Border Men turned and rode away, but the Prince stayed by the man he had thought he hated, determined not to leave him. "Get out of here, *Princeling*!" Richard said, snide and mocking to the last. He slapped the Prince's mount on the backside, sending it away. As Bleddyn reached the tree line of the next forest, he looked back. Sir Richard stood in the middle of the field, unyielding as a stone wall, his bow singing its sad song of battle and death as he shot riders from their horses. But more kept coming. Then the Prince was in the forest, and the lone Border Man was lost to sight.

Dusk was falling before their pace slowed. Bleddyn could hear the drums far away, but still too close. *I called them men without honor, and now Richard has died for us.* As they trotted up another hill, he dared to speak. "Why do they use so many drums?" He asked Khudayar as they brought up the rear.

The Arab shook his head, smiling sadly at the Prince's naïveté. "Those are not drums, my Prince. Those are the hooves of a million horses. Their riders are coming to end our world."

Bleddyn looked behind them. *Juan was right. I fear them again.* Now that it was darkening, and he had a clear view, he could see the torches. Thousands, maybe a million, spreading out in a vast river of flame. "Will we outrun them?" His voice was soft. *If I speak any louder, it will be in sobs.*

Khudayar sighed. "No, not truly. We must stand and fight."

"But not here." Jacques said. "Eyes on the horizon, my Prince."

As he circled around the trees that capped the hill, Bleddyn finally saw what they were riding towards. A river of water, not of flame, snaked across the land, far, far in the distance, glowing in the moonlight. Beyond that, however, was mass of fire, as big as the one behind. The strength of the Roman Empire was assembled, and waiting for its last great foe.

***

They forded a shallow spot in the river two days later, water splashing up to their thighs as their horses snorted water from their nostrils. Guards backed away, lowering crossbows as they recognized the group as Border Men.

"I am Sir Jacques." The old man said, voice haggard. "With me rides Bleddyn ap Maredudd, Heir to Rome and Her Territories. Where is the Emperor?"

The captain of the river guards bowed. "Well met, friends. Follow the main road until you come to a large tent with the Imperial colors. Ye can't miss it."

The war camp was so vast it took a further hour of riding to reach the Imperial command tent. Inside, all the great generals of the Roman Empire were there, analyzing their position. There was Gilchrist de Perth, Flann O'Neill, and Bleddyn's uncle, Cynfyn Mathrafal. Then there were Roland d'Anjou and Hugh Capet, Alfonso de Cantabria and Balian Guideschi, Andronikos Doukas and Belisarios Palaiologos. All the great generals and captains of the Empire. Some were counts, some were dukes, some were kings. Crusaders and cynics, strategists and sword-arms, all assembled to defend the Empire.

In their midst, he stood. Maredudd ap Gruffydd of

House Mathrafal, The Second of His Name, by the Grace of God, Emperor of Rome and Her Territories. He was a tall man with muscles as sinewy strong as his son's. His bushy brown beard was flecked with grey, but his eyes were not dulled by age. *Not yet, anyway.*

"Bleddyn!" The Emperor exclaimed, beaming broadly. "You've returned!"

"Yes, father. I have."

"Are you injured?"

"No, father." Bleddyn rarely spoke submissively to anyone but the Emperor.

The Emperor's eyes locked on Sir Jacques. "You have my thanks, Sir, for returning my son to me safely."

The old Border Man bowed. "He hardly needed saving, Your Majesty. You have trained him well. For that I am grateful. We shall all have need of strong swords and quick minds."

The Emperor nodded, his smile receding. "True enough." He motioned for them to sit. "You must be tired, my friends." They sat in empty chairs, the Prince taking the one directly facing his father's across the table.

"Bleddyn, I believe you rode in the company of five Border Men. Yet I count only four."

He felt a twinge of sadness, remembering the man they lost. *There was no love between us. I called him a man without honor.* "Yes, father;" He said, face betraying no thought, "Sir Richard of Tilton-on-the-Hill rode with us. His horse was injured in our flight, and he bade us go on without him, while he faced the Horde."

"A brave man." The Emperor said. Cruel and rough, but yes, father, brave. Though certainly not honorable by Rome's standards. "He will not be forgotten."

"Your Majesty," Sir Jacques said, "We have ridden far through harsh terrain, with the Mongols close behind. We know their movements better than your scouts in the camp. How stand the preparations?"

"The army was assembled all along the Vistula two weeks ago. Since then, the western bank has been lined with stakes all the way to the Baltic Sea, and we are digging trenches."

"Dig faster, father." Bleddyn said. "They'll be here in three days, four at most."

"Three days?" Balian Guideschi was aghast. He had a habit of being aghast, but the Prince could not blame him when it came to the Mongols.

"Or four. It doesn't matter." Bleddyn's voice was firm enough to make his father smile. "And when the Mongols come, we will show them how Roman armies fight."

Four days later, Bleddyn was woken at dawn by the thundering of drums and trumpets. His squire helped him into his armor, the finest plate-and-mail, with a magnificent helm. On it sat a crest, a gold-plated dragon wrought in steel with ruby eyes. It was all far more advanced than the light scales and leather the Border Men wore.

He and his command formed up as the first Mongols appeared on the opposite bank. His purpose in battle would be to harass the foe as they climbed onto the Roman side of the Vistula. With him would ride fifty knights. Their task was dangerous, but important. He only wished the Border Men rode with him, but they had gone to the ships on the northern coast with four hundred others like them, to circle around the Mongol Horde and harass their rear.

The Mongols were struggling to wade through the river. Arrows whistled through the air, and men screamed as they died. Bleddyn drew his sword, and he and his knights charged forward like warriors out of an old ballad. *I asked myself what good a sword is without honor wielding it.* Bleddyn thought as his blade took a man's head from his shoulders. *I have my answer.*

A sword is good for killing.

***

Twenty Years Later

The Emperor sat proud on his throne, his beautiful Empress beside him. On the dais below sat his heir, and his wife. The Imperial Court was now in session, and complaints were brought forward. The Emperor dealt with them as justly as he could. *A ruler should be just and merciful. Where he can afford to be.* His mind was not really on the proceedings, though. Instead, he observed the courtiers, standing on the sides of the throne room.

So many plots. So many plans. So many ambitions. *And here I sit, in the middle of it all.* He was the only person in the world who could keep them in check. He was the only one who could threaten anyone in the Empire, the only one who could bribe anyone in the Empire. *The only one.* The Emperor found himself thinking of the Border Men. Those he had ridden with, Jacques, Juan, Konrad, Khudayar, had all died fighting the Mongols at the Battle of the Vistula, as had his father, Maredudd, and more than a million others from both sides. *Victory at a great cost, but victory all the same.*

He had come to realize, long ago, why his father had sent him to ride with the Border Men, as he had before him, and as the new heir would soon enough. The task of the Border Men was the same as that of the Emperor. To preserve and advance the realm, by whatever means necessary. *In the end, it's just a game. Generation to generation, every dynasty plays it. And victory will not be found through honor.*

"Everything a ruler does must be for the greater good. The honor of a few is a worthy price to pay to protect the realm."

-Bleddyn ap Maredudd of House Mathrafal, The Third of His Name, By the Grace of God, Emperor of Rome and Her Territories, author of Comentarii de Dominatus, 1370 Anno Domini

***

IN ACTUAL HISTORY

The known world of *The Border Men* is dominated by two major powers. Historically, the original Bleddyn Mathrafal was a mid-11th century ruler of the Kingdom of Gwynedd in the north of what is now Wales. He is recorded as being a capable ruler, but his family never rose high in stature among the dynasties of Medieval Europe, and had died out by 1366. In this history, the Mathrafals, through centuries of marriage, inheritance, and ambition came to dominate European politics, in a similar way to our history's Capetian dynasty. The Imperial branch of the dynasty remains culturally Brittonic, keeping the many peoples of the Empire together through a Latin-based, highly centralized infrastructure. The Border Men function as a semi-autonomous branch of the military, fending off raids and scouting the horizons, waiting for the day the Mongols come.

The "Horde" featured in the story is the Golden Horde. In history, the Golden Horde was one of two western Mongolian Khanates, the other being the Ilkhanate. By 1366, the Golden Horde stretched from the Urals to the bank of the Danube, but had fallen into decline. However, in this alternate Europe, the Golden Horde continued west, conquering as far as Scandinavia, and also subjugating the territories of the Ilkhanate. The Golden Horde remains tribal in nature, a loose but fearsome collection of chieftains led by a long line of warrior-khans.

ABOUT AXEL KYLANDER

Axel Kylander is a teenager from rural Minnesota and an aspiring writer. He has taken three years of Latin and is currently studying German. When not writing historical, allegorical fiction, he partakes in many hobbies. He holds a red belt in mixed martial arts, and in the autumn enjoys the wonders of nature as he hunts. He has a passionate interest in Byzantine history, and reads about it as often as he is able. An avid gamer, *Crusader Kings II* quickly became his favorite among many candidates for that illustrious title, and he has spent over 2,000 hours playing it. "The Border Men" is based on personal experience with *Crusader Kings II*.

Axel Kylander is one of the winners of the *Crusader Kings II* Short Story Contest 2014.

THE KING

By James Mackie

The King was a disgusting man. Everybody knew it. Fat, arrogant, cruel and lecherous, his wicked character was known throughout the realm. Gisele had heard the stories, and had known what to expect even before seeing him in person. The glimpses she had caught around the castle only served to reinforce what she, and everyone else, thought of the man.

King Eduard cut a monstrous figure. Wild, black hair, unshaven, big and broad-shouldered but with a bulging pot belly, his wine-stained lips betrayed the source of his bulk. He ploughed through copious amounts of food and alcohol, and if he was not stuffing his face, then he was either laughing cruelly or arguing ferociously. His savage nature was epitomised by the long, deep scar which ran vertically across his face, the damage clouding his left eye, a relic of some old conflict decades past. Not that Eduard had been seen near a battlefield recently; Gisele doubted there would be a horse strong enough to bear his weight. The realm had seen a period of relative peace, and rumour was that Eduard had taken to sating his bloodlust by torturing the poor souls in his dungeon. Gisele shuddered at the thought.

Despite his grotesque appearance, King Eduard seemed quite vain, and Gisele had seen him preening in a mirror on a number of occasions. Maybe he had been handsome in his youth, but that was far from the case now. Of course, his lack of looks didn't stop him showing an unhealthy interest in any young female who had the misfortune to be nearby, especially since the Queen was largely absent now. It upset Gisele to think how the royal marriage vows must have been broken countless times over the years, and she couldn't grasp how such an affront to God was tolerated. When raising this in private with her family, they shook their heads, saying she was too young to understand. She knew enough to recognise weak, compromising excuses, though; excuses made to hush away discussion.

Of all the reasons to hate King Eduard, it was this change in her family's attitude which sickened her the most. Her father, Guy, was a powerful lord, ruling their extensive lands firmly but fairly. Gisele had seen her father dealing with their own vassals, diplomatic but decisive. He always acted with decorum, embodying everything which Gisele thought a noble ruler should be. Frankly, in this part of the realm, her influential family had been Kings in all but name. As a young noblewoman, she was pleased and proud of her lineage. Then, suddenly, King Eduard had come to visit. Gisele's idea of her honourable aristocracy, ruling by grace and by God, was now mocked by the sight of this slobbering, sadistic King. Not only that, but her image of an all-powerful father had been thrown out the window too, as her whole family bent the knee to these interlopers from the royal palace.

Playing host to the King's entourage had been trying at best. The castle, her beloved family home, was now filled with strange faces and scowling, unfamiliar guards. She normally enjoyed a good level of freedom, roaming both within the walls and beyond, but that had been severely curtailed, and she couldn't shake the feeling that they were all being kept prisoner. It had all felt rather unnecessary, at least until she was told the reason for the royal visit.

Today, she'd found out that the main point of discussion between her father and Eduard had been Gisele herself. Her parents said it should be flattering, but she found it anything but. She was being told to marry King Eduard's eldest son.

***

The news had felt like a blow to the stomach. Her parents had started talking about how proud they were, about how she was to become a woman, but the words had washed over Gisele's disoriented senses. Standing in the great hall, she remembered furiously biting her tongue, terrified to let her true feelings show. King Eduard himself was sitting across from her, appraising her with his one good eye, a satisfied smirk on his ugly face. Gisele wanted to scream. She did not want to be family to that man. To have to live in the same palace as him, to watch him overindulge every disgusting evening, to be constantly in fear of his feral temper… this was a nightmare. By all accounts, the son was shaping up to be like the father. She would be surrounded by those animals for the rest of her life.

Her mouth went dry and her palms were slick with sweat. Gisele knew everyone was watching her, but to reveal her true, horrified feelings would be fatal. She was too scared to talk but, mercifully, the adults were not expecting much of a discussion. Forcing her body not to tremble, she managed to mutter a quiet, demure acknowledgement. She spent the rest of that meeting in a daze, eyes fixed firmly on the floor, carefully controlling her breathing. It seemed to work, and Eduard and her parents exchanged platitudes about family bonds and building for the future. Eduard, predictably, wanted to toast the decision with yet another bottle of wine. Gisele didn't trust her shaking hands not to fumble the goblet, but somehow she brought the liquid to her lips without losing her composure, and forced the vintage down her dry throat. It was the sweetest of reds, but her nerves made the taste a disgustingly bitter one.

Eventually, she was excused. Walking normally from the great hall felt like another insurmountable challenge, but finally she found herself outside and in one piece. Gisele wanted to break down and cry, but there was still too much risk that one of the royal entourage would see her, and everything now depended on maintaining appearances. The young noblewoman wandered the corridors with apparent aimlessness, still reeling from the life-ruining events of the day.

Slowly, she gathered her senses, and she could start to think more rationally about the situation. Gisele was at least grateful for the fact that she had kept her nerve back in the hall. Collapsing or bursting into tears would have been unforgivably childish and drawn stern rebuke. At least now, the older generation would think she intended to go along with their plans, which just might give her the breathing room needed to put a stop to them.

Awakening from her daze and looking around her, she realised she had drifted across the courtyard, her legs taking her to the stables. She smiled wryly as she realised what her troubled mind must have been thinking. Tempting as it would be to steal a horse and ride into the sunset, away from the horrors of King Eduard, she knew that wasn't a practical option, not least because the royal guards had her father's castle firmly under their control. It was hopeless to think that what little freedom she had would extend past the walls or gate.

However, as she stood to the side of the bustling stables, Gisele started to see more subtle solutions to her problem. Perhaps the only advantage of playing host to the royal entourage, her family home being overrun with soldiers meant that the stables and storerooms were a lot busier than usual. Put-upon staff were hurrying around, with control over supplies that little bit more chaotic. It was no problem at all for the petite Gisele to weave through the throng, quietly acquiring a length of rope and hiding it in the folds of her dress.

The successful theft gave her a small buzz of excitement. It was a minor victory, but it meant that escape was no longer so implausible. Her mind was whirring now, as she began to plan out what she needed to do. She spent the next couple of hours drifting around the castle as inconspicuously as possible, quietly acquiring the vitals she would need. Bread and dried meat, that was easy enough. Ink and parchment were relatively unguarded, too. Next, a dagger from the blacksmiths. Obtaining the weapon was more of a challenge, but again, the increased bustle of foreign soldiers wanting their swords sharpened proved to be a helpful distraction. Gisele chuckled at the irony, as the self-important royal guard unknowingly let her by, a small but dangerous threat passing right under their noses. The young noblewoman carefully concealed the dagger, emboldened and reassured by the cold metal hidden against her body.

She was doing well. Her illicit acquisitions had not attracted any unwanted attention. All she had to do now was retire to her chambers in the main keep and wait for night to fall. It was the tail end of summer, so this took longer than she would have liked, but it meant that the castle descended into a warm, still, pleasant darkness, stars shining prettily though gaps in the moonlit cloud. A nice night, and perfect for what she planned to do.

In her room, Giselle was getting changed, ostensibly for dinner, but she knew better than the adults. Instead of her evening gown, she had dismissed her maids and was pulling on a far more practical outfit. One of the King's men was guarding her door, but she had an alternate exit in mind, one that would outwit that foreign dolt.

She took a few deep breaths to settle her nerves as she looked ahead to what she needed to do, making a mental checklist. Rope to escape from her window down to the wall. From there, escape should be easy enough, as the castle was designed to keep people out, not in. Home knowledge helped her out, she knew plenty of places where the dirt piled against the ramparts was high enough to comfortably break someone's fall. The main risk was being seen from the towers as she covered the grassland between the wall and the forest. It would be a dangerous dash, for sure, but the darkness should protect her, and once she reached the cover of the trees she would be safe.

It was time. Strangely, she didn't feel any fear over what she was doing. Probably because this night-time escape was far less terrifying than the prospect of staying put. Taking matters into her own hands, rather than passively accepting the orders of her elders, felt surprisingly good. Gisele didn't think of herself as a rebel, and she was sad about going against her family like this, but ultimately she needed to keep some control over events. What she was about to do could rattle the entire Kingdom, but she knew it was for the best.

Fastening one end of the rope to her heavy wooden bed, she unfurled the remaining length out of the window, creating an escape route. She looked anxiously down, scanning for sentries, but they seemed entirely absent from her corner of the wall. Definitely a piece of luck, and a good omen. She did not want to tangle with a guard, but had resolved to use the dagger if she had to. With a deep breath, the nimble girl grabbed the rope and swung herself out of the window.

Gisele was athletic enough to clamber down the wall with relative ease, feet against the stonework supporting her weight as the rappelled down the rope. The course weave hurt the palms of her hands, but she would rather be quick than comfortable. If anyone caught her while she was dangling from her window, she would have a tough time of it indeed.

Fortunately, she reached the bottom with speed, and dropped quietly onto the main castle wall. She was confident that she hadn't made a noise, and couldn't see a single guard. All she needed to do now was find a low spot to drop from the battlement. She began to scuttle along the top of the wall.

"Stop right there!" an angry voice called out from behind her. Gisele froze in fear, her heightened senses shocked at this unwelcome development. A foreign-sounding voice, marking him out as one of the King's own guard. He must have been patrolling round the far side of the tower, with Gisele dropping into view at the most unfortunate time. He took advantage of her hesitation, Gisele hearing a couple of footsteps before a hand came down on her shoulder.

The noblewoman's blood ran cold at the powerful grip on her arm. She was too scared to look round. The guard, for his part, saw that she was paralysed with fear… but that assumption was wrong. Gisele was afraid to turn around, yes, but only because she knew that it would be far easier not to see the face of someone she was about to kill.

The dagger at her waist could be reached quickly and easily. From her frozen position, her hand shot down and grasped the handle, pulling it up before swinging it fiercely back behind her, stabbing blindly at the man.

With his hand on her shoulder, the guard had no defence. However, he felt the muscle movement in Gisele's right arm, giving him forewarning of her sudden attack. He instinctively pushed the girl to the side and recoiled backwards.

"Agh!" the guard exclaimed as the dagger swung towards his stomach, missing him by a fraction of an inch. If he hadn't given Gisele that push, he would be dead.

Gisele herself was dismayed to feel her dagger swipe

at empty air. Surprise was her only advantage against this foe and she had largely squandered it. Guided by pure adrenaline and fierce intent, she pulled the blade up and spun gracefully around, looking right into the man's face before plunging the dagger down, straight into the centre of his chest.

The guard stared down, open-mouthed. His chain mail had stopped the blow, saving his life. Fortunately for him, the petite girl had elected for an overarm swing, the best she could do in the circumstances, but the angle and power of the blade had not been enough to penetrate his armour. As a royal guard, he had the best equipment. A lesser lookout would be dead.

Now Gisele froze in horror, for real this time, as she was caught mid-stab. The man's astonished features hardened into an angry snarl, hands coming up to grab Gisele's wrist and tear the small weapon from her grasp. He glared down at her, eyes darkening, adrenaline pumping from his brush with death.

He spat some foreign curse, holding Gisele by her arms and giving her a violent shake. He clearly wanted to kill her. They were alone on the battlements, he could easily dash her head against the wall, or throw her from the rampart to look like a horrible accident.

Fear flooded Gisele's senses. She squirmed in an attempt to claim her arms back from the man, but it was utterly futile. Half her opponent's size, she was in serious trouble, and utterly at his mercy. He yanked her wrist sharply, pulling her stumbling towards his body, where he wrapped an arm around her and lifted her up off her feet.

Gisele was badly disoriented now as she was slung roughly across the man's shoulder, her legs dangling uselessly in the air, her hands trapped by the controlling arm around her waist. The situation was bad enough now that she figured she should cut her losses and begin calling for help, but the guard clamped his free hand over her nose and mouth. The rest of the darkness-shrouded castle would remain oblivious to Gisele's predicament.

The guard turned around. Gisele, hanging helplessly over his shoulder, found her head swinging out towards the edge of the wall. She could see straight down to the bottom of the battlements, a vertiginous, sickening sight, undoubtedly deadly if her captor decided to throw her over. She whimpered in fear as she contemplated the drop, but it seemed the guard had other plans. He marched to the tower door, holding the mute, trembling girl across his shoulder, and began climbing the stairs to Gisele's room.

Up the spiral they went. Sick with nerves, Gisele had abandoned all hope of escape. Now her only aim was survival. She knew they were back at her bedroom when she heard the door sentry splutter in shock, obviously appalled to see his charge both outside the room, and in the clutches of another guard. The two of them conversed urgently in hushed tones, Gisele barely understanding the rough dialect of the capital.

Now it was two against one, Gisele knew better than to even try and resist. She wasn't sure what the men had decided, but they carried her into her room and unceremoniously dumped her onto her bed. Tears spilled from her eyes as she tried to come to terms with what was happening.

The door guard swore when he saw the rope hanging from the window. Muttering to themselves, but moving efficiently, they gathered the rope back up, before dragging Gisele's trembling form over to a chair.

She had already abandoned her plans of escape, but this hopelessness was reinforced when they began to tie her to the chair, the poor girl bound up with her own rope.

"You need to stay put now," the door sentry said gruffly as he looped the rope around his captive. The other guard was milling around the room, clearly struggling to suppress his anger at the situation, having almost been stabbed, but he remained silent. Evidently, Gisele's noble blood was protecting her from harm, but she didn't know how long that would last.

"Stay and be quiet. I think we need to speak to the King," the first man told Gisele as he finished knotting the rope, leaving her strapped to the chair. He escorted his seething friend to the door, then the pair left the room, closing the door firmly behind them.

Alone in her chamber again, Gisele burst into more tears, unable to contain the stress any longer. The day was going from bad to worse, and she was left in dreadful anticipation of what would happen to her now. She was still in shock from her altercation with the guards, and although she had come out of it unscathed, there would surely be punishment to follow. As an important noblewoman she could expect some protection, but the matter had been contained by the King's guards, rather than her own father's. If she was lucky, her family would hear of what had happened and get involved, and whilst she would still be in severe trouble, she would at least have a chance of being treated fairly. Of course, if she was unlucky, then the brutish King Eduard would come to deal with the problem himself.

The trapped girl didn't know how long she spent on

the chair, alone with her fearful thoughts, but the tears on her cheeks dried, and she managed to get her nervous trembling under control. She had no option but to take what was coming, and face it with dignity. Still, she jumped when the door creaked open again, and her heart froze when she saw who it was.

The king. Alone. He closed the door behind him and fixed her with a hard stare. As much as Gisele wanted to remain defiant, the King's ugly, scarred visage made his gaze impossible to meet. She turned away in fear and shame.

"I'm sorry," he sighed. "They shouldn't have tied you up."

Gisele frowned a little in confusion as the King began to walk over to her. She wasn't sure what was happening.

"I trust that, if I untie you, you won't be so foolish as to hurl yourself out of the window?" he asked.

Gisele just mumbled, bewildered and uncomprehending, as the King, apparently in good spirits, started to unfasten the knots in the rope.

"Yes, I know, silly idea. Not sure what those men were thinking, they could have just left you in here without all this unpleasantness. I suppose you might have rattled them with that dagger," he chuckled to himself. "In fact, you nearly made fools of both of them, but at least they had the good sense to come straight to me. No need to worry, Gisele, no-one else has heard about this."

He pulled the rope away and then sat down on the edge of the bed. Gisele, aware she was being watched but unsure what was expected of her, nervously stretched her arms and massaged her shoulder, slightly stiff from where she had been held. She swallowed hard, watching the king carefully. She was apparently free, but she knew she had to remain extremely cautious. There was no guarantee that her life would not be forfeit.

"I…you must be angry. Please, believe me, I am truly sorry," she began. "What I did…I know it was disrespectful, but I will make amends, I swear."

"Ah, now, why would I be angry?" Eduard replied, a sly grin across his unshaven face.

What game was he playing? Gisele wondered if the King was already drunk, to the point of confusion or memory loss. It was the most compelling explanation for the fact that the wayward noblewoman was still in one piece.

"I…well…I…tried to run away…attacked that man…" she stammered.

"Oh, I think we'll put that one down to self-defence," the King smiled indulgently. "Besides, there can't be many princesses that quick with a knife. I'm impressed!"

Gisele wasn't a princess, and she opened her mouth to make that point, before realising the subtle hint. Her marriage to the prince was still very much on the table, despite all that had happened.

"It was more than just running away though, wasn't it? Come on, be honest with me," the King continued. "Talk me through it."

"Um, okay," Gisele swallowed. This could still be a ploy to get her to incriminate herself, before the true, savage nature of the King, which she had been expecting, came to the fore. Although if that was the case, she was going to be in trouble anyway. She might as well gamble on honesty being the best policy, for once.

"I had two days' worth of supplies," she began. "I

could have made it to the next town on foot, I know the terrain well. I know the local lord well, too. All the nobles here are loyal to my father," she said proudly.

"And…" the King prodded for more. It was clear now that he knew the full extent of her plan.

"They were expecting me," sighed Gisele, unhappy that she had to confess her full betrayal. "I knew I could offer my hand in marriage to one of their sons, and get their support. They would have protected me, stopped me being taken back to the capital."

A horrible thought suddenly struck Gisele. "My father is innocent!" she added urgently. "None of my family know anything about this! I was acting alone!"

"I know," Eduard held his hands up, placating her. "Don't worry, I know. I found the message you were trying to send out to the neighbours. One of my hunters shot down the bird you snuck out, brought it straight to me. No ducal seal, plus it didn't really strike me as your father's style, so I thought I could probably guess the culprit."

Gisele held a hand to her forehead in embarrassment. She felt silly having been caught sending a message for help out like that. "I thought it best to prepare them… I still needed them to expect a noblewoman, which would be tricky after I'd spent two days trudging through the woods on foot, dressed like a peasant."

"No, you were probably right to," Eduard deferred. "It would almost make your plan legitimate. I know most of the locals round here believe the stories about me, so it wouldn't take much to trigger an uprising," he sighed. "To be honest, you were unlucky to have your bird caught like that. If it hadn't, I wouldn't have known to put extra men on you this evening."

Gisele pursed her lips together ruefully. She thought

it had seemed unlucky that sentry was right behind her after scaling down the wall. However, these details obscured a bigger mystery—why was King Eduard pleasantly picking over strategy, when, by all accounts, he should be blind with rage? She had to confess, he had won the battle of wits—but his reputation suggested he would have solved this with his fists.

She couldn't bear the suspense any longer, she had to address it. "Are you…going to punish me?" she cringed. Thoughts of the rumoured torture victims in the dungeons of the capital flashed unwillingly across her eyes.

"What? No! Why?" the King exclaimed. "I'm pleased! You're marrying my son and, by all accounts, will make an excellent bride for him. I'll be honest, we were mainly interested in the dowry, and we could do with better relations in this part of the realm, but you actually seem like good Queen material, too!"

Gisele still looked a little bewildered, so Eduard spelled it out. "I mean, look—some children throw tantrums and run away from home. But you plan ahead and sow a small rebellion to cover your tracks! I really did have no idea, you hid your reaction in the great hall earlier with great skill. I wish half of the idiots in this realm had that subtlety!" he laughed. "Well, maybe not, it makes them so much easier to rule as it is."

"So what have you shown me?" he continued. "You're intelligent, forward-thinking, resourceful, not too shabby with a dagger, apparently… I've no doubt you'll keep my son in shape when he takes over the throne."

Gisele was beginning to understand. A greater truth was dawning on her, as well. "You're a smart man…but all the stories about your…brutality…"

Eduard smiled, perhaps a little smug, but his eyes were twinkling. "People like to talk. If it suits me, I let them. The scary monster rampaging round with an iron fist, it seems to be working. It's kept the peace for years. There's a good reason I've not had to go to war for a while. I don't even know how it started... I think it's the eye." Eduard motioned to his scarred face. "People think I look evil... but I'm the one that got stabbed in the face! How does that make me the villain?" He chuckled to himself, looking over to Gisele. Now that he mentioned it, she realised it did seem pretty absurd. She smiled along with him.

"So I'm fighting to defend my own realm, I happen to get on the wrong end of a sword, and I end up some kind of fairytale monster. I would have quashed it, but it kept everyone in line after the war. A useful story."

"I think it works," Gisele nodded.

"Well, it helps the realm, it helps the family. You're kin now, too...so let me know if I'm overdoing it. I might get carried away after the wine starts to flow..." he chuckled.

Gisele felt a wave of relief. It seemed there were no overstocked torture chambers at the royal palace, no reign of terror, just a smart man playing a role that had been picked out for him. Something that she would be doing in the not too distant future. At least she would be learning from the best.

"So, where do I fit into all this? How exactly do I keep your son—the future King—in line?"

Eduard grinned. "Oh, you don't keep him in line. He's a royal! His word will be law! But...if he's surrounded by enough intelligent people, making the right suggestions at the right times, then with any luck, his decisions might actually be good ones."

THE KING – JAMES MACKIE

"Look, I'm not going to lie, the lad is more interested in drinking and jousting than playing politics. He's not a bad soul though, he can be the 'chivalrous prince' if we keep him on the right path. Should be easy, with a pretty princess on his arm, who's well-connected in the right parts of the realm, and seems to understand the darker arts of diplomacy."

Gisele nodded demurely. "And of course, give him a son as soon as possible."

"Heh, didn't need to tell you that, did I?" Eduard continued. "Though I'm probably not the best person to be handing out advice. Only married the Queen because we needed her family's troops…probably the nicest thing I can say about her, to be honest. Take care of your kin, though, and it'll work out all right."

He slapped his knees and stood up with purpose.

"Right! I'm off downstairs to be a drunken terror. You'd better get ready damned quickly, and come down for dinner like nothing ever happened. Which I already know you are very good at," he winked, heading for the door.

Gisele let out a long, deep breath. It would be easy to be stunned by the revelations and level of deception, that her whole Kingdom was being held together by various lies and ruses. Already, though, the wheels of her brain were turning, planning what was needed for the evening ahead, the upcoming months, the wedding preparations and how to deal with the other lords of the realm.

Irritatingly, the King was completely right. She didn't need to be a good person, but she was going to be a good Queen.

***

IN ACTUAL HISTORY

The early medieval growth of the Frankish realm, followed by the Norman expansions of the 11th century, left most of western Europe under a Francophone nobility and a common feudal system. From Scotland to Sicily, a shared courtly culture and web of marriage alliances spanned the continent. For these entrenched, land-owning elites, family and politics were one and the same, and betrothals and marriages were absolutely key. The above story isn't tied to a particular place in the pan-European system, and could have occurred anywhere. Children were placed in arranged marriages for political gain and this was absolutely normal, personal considerations were largely ignored.

With feudal system revolving around such a small number of families and personalities, the politics of an entire country could be influenced by the ruler's spouse. It is not known to what extent rulers would be able to pick the best candidates, sadly lacking the specific bride-finding tools available to *Crusader Kings II* players.

ABOUT JAMES MACKIE

Born in Scotland, I had the dubious pleasure of growing up in the most nondescript part of England possible, the Midlands (so good they named it once, and unimaginatively so). Fortunately this left plenty of time to play historical strategy games, which in turn fed into an interest in history, and ultimately obtaining a degree in it. That's why you should never listen to people who say computer games are bad. Or that playing them doesn't count as studying. Or that a degree should require more than two hours a week of work.

In the end, it transpired that educated-sounding opinions without hard data or actual facts is what most of the western economy is built on. Gainfully employed in financial services, and happily married (without needing to use the bride finder)—the only drawback being, of course, that free time to play historical strategy games gets harder to come by.

Now disappointingly English, the only remaining Celtic heritage I have involves being terrible at football, but really good at drinking whisky.

James Mackie is one of the winners of the *Crusader Kings II* Short Story Contest 2014.

THE PASSION OF GRIMSBY

By Joseph Sharp

His instructions were clear: investigate the dreadful circumstances by which his predecessor, the late Father Cuthberht, had given up the ghost while at the same time continuing the priest's mission of proselytization to the local inhabitants of Grimsby. Nasty business, the Cuthberht affair, as it had come to be called in the halls of St. Mary's in Lincoln. It began with the ominous appearance of Father Cuthberht's horse at the gates of the alien priory at Covenham, some fifteen miles south of Grimsby. What the French monks found upon closer inspection was the good father's lifeless body, completely naked, bound obscenely along the underside of his mare; his limbs, however, dangled freely, giving the horse, at first glance, the physique of an eight-legged creature. The High Sheriff of Lincolnshire, a personal enemy of the bishop, declared the incident, and not without a touch of insinuation that the man had strapped himself to the animal, a freak equestrian misadventure. Thus it became a delicate matter solely in the hands of the diocese to sort out and, of utmost importance, clear Father Cuthberht's soiled name before the slanderous news could spread any further.

Such is how the young but determined Father Thomas, summarily dispatched in the autumn of 1089, found himself standing in a sidewinding downpour watching the carriage that had borne him to this wet country wobble away into the dark. The inebriated coachman, resisting the steady building of courage known to men thigh-deep in their cups, had grabbed the priest's belongings and dropped them in the muddy road and answered the tremulous query, "Is this Grimsby?" with, "It's as near it as I'm willing to go." Father Thomas, stifling a sigh, slung his bag over his shoulder, reached for his heavy trunk, and trudged eastward along the road. The night flashed with lightning squiggling frantically over a geography momentarily revealed to include flooded fields and, in the distance, the wart of a hilltop. A crosswind howled by, peeling back the hood of his drenched cloak, revealing a ruddy and hairless face with a nose that presently wrinkled, for it could smell rotten eggs on the wind courtesy of a nearby salt marsh. Soon the wind died but the howling remained and it took the priest a moment to realize a wet and vocally adept dog splashed in the puddles alongside and now ahead, pausing, looking back at him without much interest, as if the spectacle of a clergyman trundling up a waterlogged backroad in the middle of the night was no spectacle at all. He hastened to follow it but in his rush felt his foot vacate a shoe. By the time he prized the footwear out of the mud and reattached it to the appropriate appendage the dog had run off, swallowed by the dark. As he listened to the inarticulate thunder, the crucifix that hung from his neck had at that moment more in common with a gravestone.

What he'd taken for thunder was in fact the rumble of a river. A thatch-roofed bridge spanned the burgeoning River Freshney, the churning water lapping at the bottom planks, the whole thing swaying dangerously. Thomas approached it not without a little trepidation, feeling even at a distance the peril of its hopeless dance. But then he saw the dog shaking its fur beneath the shelter of the roof. It turned and vanished and reappeared suddenly on the other side of the river. Nine-tenths of trust in the Lord, Thomas thought, clutching his crucifix with newfound pluck, that's all one needs. And, with the handle of the trunk firmly gripped, he crossed the bridge to the other side where awaited the town of Grimsby.

It appeared before him, a squalid, tightly-packed collection of ramshackle huts that looked as if they were conspiring in their proximity to one another. Thomas looked for sign of inn or church or even a stable, anywhere he might get dry, but the town offered nothing but barred doors along its muddy arteries. As he turned a corner he came across what served as the town square, such as it was—a mud-covered plaza, crisscrossed with the convenience of narrow planks that were also, for their part, covered in mud. At the center stood a stone fountain and hunkered over its overflowing rim was the lower half of a shriveled old man. Father Thomas, thinking the man drowned, approached by one of the boards, but as he came abreast of the fountain the old man pushed away from the stone rim and gasped for breath. Long grey hair matched his long grey beard, both of them sopping wet, but most striking was his affliction: he had but one eye, an imbecilic eye that now focused on the priest standing next to him.

"Excuse me," Thomas said, speaking loudly over the din of the storm. "Might you know where I can find the former residence of…"

The old man, obviously unversed in the ways of polite conversation, brayed like a jackass, then fled through the mud and vanished between two nearby huts.

The priest repositioned the bag over his shoulder, reached for his trunk, and continued on his way. He'd been told beforehand that the locals were of Danish descent and that they'd opted to retain, where matters of spiritual counsel were concerned, the beliefs of their ancestors. This, his instructions emphasized, was not only to be discouraged, but also subjected to intense scrutiny with regards to the Cuthberht affair. That Norsemen might be responsible for the murder was beyond question; it only remained to find out which of them had done the deed.

At the easternmost end of town he discovered a dilapidated building with no door. Its roof, what had once been nicely steepled, now kept the floor company in a mazelike heap of stone rubble. And there, jutting out of the top of the heap, was a broken cross.

***

He woke to the abatement of one storm and the beginning of another, for as he regained his senses he realized that the dog he'd met on the outskirts had its leg hiked and was urinating on his head. Beyond the dog, a gangly redheaded chap who seemed vaguely amused by the situation leaned against the church doorway. Thomas had in the night crawled beneath an outcrop of rubble for shelter and did not have much room with which to retreat, and his attempts to fend off the tenaciously micturating beast proved futile. "Might this be your pet, then?" he inquired.

The redhead made no indication of having heard and Thomas was about to ask him for help in restraining the animal but for the sudden cessation of waterworks. The mutt let its leg down and loped out of the church and the redhead turned to follow it.

After mopping his face with his muddied cassock, Thomas leapt up and passed through the church doorway and out into a brisk grey morning. He found the redhead ambling along toward the town square where around the stone fountain now congregated a handful of languid individuals, all of them nude and in the process of bathing. A haggard woman with stringy hair and sagging breasts glanced at him and then blew her nose into the fountain just as a broad-shouldered Norseman leaned down and submerged his face. The yard filled with the sounds of men hawking up loogies and depositing them in the fountain while others, some of them oddly bereft of nose, dunked filthy towels into the water and then sponged their inflamed crotches. The idiotic one-eyed man he'd seen in the night was continuously slapping the palm of his hands into the water while favoring in turn each fellow bather with his daft smirk.

Thomas, horrified, went up to the redhead who, at the moment, was unbuckling the belt that went around his knee-length tunic. The dog snarled at his approach.

"Pardon," Thomas said, keeping a wary eye on the

mutt, "but before you undress and do, ah, whatever it is the rest of them are doing, could you perchance explain what's happened to the church?"

The redheaded man pulled his tunic over his head, dropped it in the mud, and stood there scratching his privates. "You a doctor?" he said in a garbled but decipherable accent.

"Sorry, no, I'm a priest."

"My condolences," the man said with a frown while continuing to scratch the mangled curl of red that was his crotch, then muttered, "Could've used a doctor."

"Yes, well, as I was saying, the church seems to have fallen into a rather unfortunate state of disrepair…"

The redheaded man shrugged. "Faulty masonry. We're not miracle workers. Only so much you can do in this awful fenland. I told him from the start, a big stone building like that would never stay up."

"You're speaking of Father Cuthberht?"

"That's the one. Refused to compromise."

"How do you mean?"

"Wood. Wood is pliable. It agrees with the earth's suggestions."

"Yes, I see," Thomas lied, "but about Father Cuthberht, you wouldn't happen to know how it is he came by his, ah, fate, would you?"

"He was a lonely man," the redhead said, joining the others in laving the fountain's gruel over his splotchy body. "Fond of horses."

Their laughter followed him back to the church.

***

That night Father Thomas found himself tormented by a dream in which an enormous tree grew high over the town, its roots penetrating the huts and the ruins of the church, but then its vibrant leaves, which were many, began to fall and wither, and the trunk, what had been strong, now deteriorated—all seemingly a byproduct of a most peculiar miracle: the church was restoring itself, stone by stone, severing the root of the dying tree.

Over the next month, compelled by this vision, he had managed on his own to clear out the church and fashion something approaching a roof out of the scrap. It looked respectable enough, and on the day he climbed his makeshift ladder to the makeshift roof to fix upon it his makeshift cross, a crowd gathered to watch. Although the cross sat askew, Thomas nonetheless gazed proudly at its crooked splendor. Then he turned to address his audience.

"Good morning," he began. "My name, as I'm sure most of you already know, is Father Thomas. I hope you might all come to look upon me as a sort of spiritual guide, a lighthouse, if you will, standing high above the confusing waters of assimilation, unmovable, unshakeable, un-*achgh*!" he screamed as he fell suddenly through the roof.

The villagers dispersed in a gas of pleased muttering. Only the redheaded man, who Thomas had come to know as Halvdan, poked his head through the church doorway. He looked up at the hole in the roof and at the priest sitting stunned on the floor.

"Man's folly," he said, "is the path to ruin."

Thomas's eyes widened. "You've just quoted the Bible."

"Faith is folly."

"And, in addition to being rude, you've inadvertently finished the proverb."

"I enjoy flyting as much as being thorough. Incidentally, has anyone told you that your face is silly?"

"Please leave."

"Very well."

***

He spent the following week visiting with each villager in turn. He learned that the woman he'd seen at the fountain, apparently the only woman in town, was called Sigrid. She sat on a stool in her hut chewing seductively on a strand of hay.

"Do you know about Jesus Christ?" he asked her.

She smiled at him, which he took as an encouraging sign.

"Well, as you are most probably aware, Jesus is our Lord and Savior. He sacrificed himself on the cross to save…"

Her legs came apart, the hem of her dress hiking up over her knees, revealing her cotton drawers. She touched a finger to her mouth.

"To save…oh, my," said Thomas. "Please, don't do that." When he reached forward to restore her modesty she lurched off her stool and grabbed him and the two of them sprawled to the floor in an oafish entanglement of limbs. Thomas, having never in his life enjoyed the warmth of a good woman, nor even a mediocre one, was at that moment a man distilled to his basest self, his celibacy vows merely an artifact of an imprudent past, such that his hand began to awkwardly probe up her drawers, feeling her chancrous inner thigh upon which swelled a colony of septic pustules, and thinking, for whatever reason, of those fountain bathers and their inflamed, rash-covered—

"Oh, my God, what am I doing?" he cried, and after extricating himself from the woman he fled the hut and smoothed his hair while casting wild glances up and down the road.

Next he paid visit, accompanied by Halvdan, who, despite earlier misgivings, served as translator, to Eirik, the broad-shouldered Norseman. His hut, one of the larger ones in Grimsby, was home to a pair of goats that trembled with fear when Eirik so much as twitched a muscle. Collected in one of the corners of the room, beneath a large hammer mounted on the wall, was a pile of animal bones that Thomas tried his best to ignore.

"Ask him if he's ever read this," he told Halvdan while holding out a leather-bound Bible.

Halvdan looked at the book. He looked at Thomas. Then he turned and spoke to Eirik in what sounded like a calm, diplomatic tone, but when he finished Eirik stood from his chair, seized Thomas by the throat, and escorted him unkindly out the door.

"What did you say to him?" the priest asked Halvdan as they walked to the next house.

"Only what you asked me to. Although I did stipulate that it was you who insisted on offending him, that I was only relaying the message."

"*Offending* him? How did I offend him?"

Halvdan shrugged. "He doesn't know how to read."

They stood before the next hut. As Thomas reached forward to knock, Halvdan touched his shoulder, stopping him.

"Maybe we ought to skip this one."

"Why? Who lives here?"

"Canute."

"The one-eyed idiot?"

"The same."

"What happened to him? Was he in a battle?"

"No, nothing of the sort," Halvdan said. "In an attempt to emulate Odin, he plucked his own eyeball out and dropped it into the fountain, believing that in so doing he would be granted great wisdom. Obviously he regrets the whole affair, as he spends most of his time trying to fetch it back."

"Oh, my. That's horrible. But, regardless, I think it best I meet with the man. We're all of us God's children, after all."

"If you say so."

When Thomas knocked on the door it creaked open an inch. His greeting met with silence. He reached forward and prodded the door open a little more, a blade of dull light stabbing into a dark, earthen lair. Thomas gulped. He glanced over at Halvdan, who had crossed the road and sat himself on a barrel, where he rather looked like a man ready for the theatre curtains to open.

"Are you coming?" Thomas said.

Halvdan shook his head.

"Right." Thomas turned back to the door and opened it the rest of the way. "Hello? Canute?" He stepped over the threshold onto a clay floor. The room was cold and smelled of cabbage and the light from outside was little help in illuminating anything other than a strange series of scrimshawed idols that hung from the thatched roof by clipped strands of vine. "Canute?"

A strong breeze stole the door shut. Thomas whirled, nearly screaming. He started for the door but his feet stayed their place. An odd slurping sound reached his ears. The sound morphed suddenly into a bird squawk and when Thomas finally made a panicked go for the door he discerned some shape rising out of the dark and blocking his way.

The idiot stood before him, squawking.

"Canute?" Thomas said, not caring for the way his voice cracked.

The squawking stopped. Canute took a step forward. His presence, although withered from age, seemed to dominate the entire room. Thomas closed his eyes, preparing for the worst.

"Bonjour," the idiot said.

***

Father Thomas learned a very important lesson that day: *Idiots surprise.* What a marvelous idiot, the priest thought as he watched Canute scrape a sizzling chunk of beef off a frying pan and onto his waiting plate. Not only did the fool speak perfectly good Norse, but was also fluent in both French and English. A trilingual idiot! Whatever will God think of next?

And it was God that became the primary topic of discussion for their lunch. Canute sat in stupid wonder, soaking up every bit of information that poured from Thomas's mouth about the strange singular deity. He listened as Thomas regaled him with the origins of the earth and of its living creatures that swam the depths of the seas and flew the heights of the sky and of the first man that God made in His image to have dominion over all that creeps and slithers and swims and soars.

"Wait," he interrupted. "Man comes from dust?"

"Yes," said Thomas.

"But it's my understanding that man was made from the hardy wood of an ash tree."

"That's the most ridiculous thing I've ever heard. Man made from a tree, come on. If we were made from wood we'd walk around like this," and here Father Thomas stood from his stool and made a show of walking stiffly, arms and legs locked straight, around the hut.

Canute, pleased, as idiots are wont to be when encountering such theatrics, rose himself and ambled over to a shelf where he ran his finger along its rough surface. Then he came back and sat down and showed his dust-covered finger to Thomas. "Is this what we're made of?"

"That's what the Bible says."

"A man made of dust is a dusty man," Canute said. He blew the dust from his finger. "And such is a dusty man's fate." He leaned forward and blew in Thomas's face, then leaned back smugly in his chair.

"Very astute, Canute. But I'm afraid you're forgetting something."

"What's that?"

"That God, in His infinite wisdom, packed us tightly and sturdily with a special kind of dust, for when God touches something, it becomes more than it would otherwise appear."

"So you're saying that God, who created everything, including dust, can additionally imbue his creations, by touch, with magical properties?"

"Yes."

"Can he give me back my eye?"

"No."

"Why not?"

"It just doesn't work that way."

"But did Jesus not restore the sight and hearing and even, on occasion, the lives of men?"

227

Impressive, Thomas thought. He belongs in a circus! Why, they'd queue up for leagues for a chance to see this spectacular idiot! "You know more than you let on, Canute, and your argument, while insolent, has nonetheless managed to persuade me. Yes, I don't see why the Good Lord would begrudge a simpleton like you a single eyeball. All we need do is pray."

***

Before Father Thomas left, Canute asked if he could borrow the Bible so that he might better understand its so-called Good News, and the priest was more than happy to oblige. For the first time since he arrived in Grimsby he felt invigorated. He'd managed the impossible, the hook was baited, and, provided he play his cards right, Father Thomas was on the verge of catching his first fish.

What better way to end a busy day of proselytizing than to curl up on the cot in the back of the church and while away the rest of the evening with his favorite book? Drat, he thought, remembering that his Bible was currently being drooled upon by the idiot. How easily we find grief even in our victories. Without the Good Book to keep him company he found his thoughts drawn to darker climes, to, more specifically, the Cuthberht affair. He sat on the cot, wondering if perhaps the man had simply lost his mind. No, it couldn't be. A clergyman in congress with a horse? Surely not, God would never allow it. But then, technically, in the end, God *didn't* allow it, did He? Oh, dear, he thought, and with his subconscious working overtime to distract him from spoiling his good mood, he looked at the grimy stone floor. Although he'd cleared out the rubble, he had yet to get personal with the details, to apply, as they say, a little elbow grease. He went outside with a bucket to the fountain, reconsidered the wisdom of cleaning a floor with that unearthly concoction, and instead made a trip down to the river. When he returned he upended the bucket over the church floor and set to work scrubbing each individual stone. In paying close attention to the grout as he worked his way from the entrance of the church to the transept, he came across a loose stone, and, after prying it up, extracted a hidden diary.

"What have we here?" he said aloud, opening the small book. He skimmed through it, the staid and frankly boring catalogue of a repressed priest, from his arrival in Grimsby to the construction of the church and his frustrated attempts to deliver the townsfolk into Christ's bosom, but then, as Thomas read further, the tone changed abruptly, an edge of danger swept through the bland moorland of Cuthberht's daily life. "'I've come to enjoy my sessions with Sigrid, she seems, more than any here, to grasp and understand my troubles…'" and here Thomas's eyes scanned the next page, "'…the locals say, quite crudely, that she spreads all eight of her legs for any who'd wish to ride her, horrible, I'd kill them all if I could, especially her father, that carrot-headed cur, disparaging my beloved Sigrid like that.'" Thomas wanted nothing more than to close the book, to forget it ever existed, but he could not resist turning to the final page, where he read: "'…I've determined to forsake my flock, my vows, for the sake of love, for my dear and beautiful Sigrid, with whom I shall flee Grimsby this very night…'"

Resolutely, no half-measures, he took the diary over

to the votive candles beneath a rejiggered statue of Jesus affixed to his cross and set the book to the flames. "Don't give me that look," he told Christ, and in turn heard a response, What look? "The one you're giving me right now, of disapproval." Well, how else would you have me look upon your actions, with endorsement? "Of course not, I know what I'm doing is wrong, but it's wrong for all the right reasons." Oh, the things we tell ourselves. "I'm protecting your Church." You're protecting the interests of the bishop. "Well, who pays my stipend, you, or the bishop?" For someone so young you sure are cynical, why did you even join the clergy? "If you must know, I was volunteered by my father, the Earl of Lincoln. He wanted to keep the line of succession pure—his word—for my younger but slightly more legitimate brother, Todd." That's the most pathetic thing I've ever heard. "Be quiet." Don't tell me to be quiet, I'm the Son of God, I suffered for your sins. "You're the son of arrogance. Plenty of men have suffered worse than you, ever heard of the blood eagle?" You are walking a fine line, young man. "I don't want to talk to you anymore, go away." This is my house, you go away. "Fine, I will," and here Father Thomas disengaged from this altogether unhealthy tête-à-tête. He dropped the burning diary in the mud outside and wept as its secrets shriveled to ash.

***

In the weeks that followed, Father Thomas, who held Mass in the restored church every Sunday morning, noticed with delight his congregation growing more and more until finally, on one fateful day, there wasn't an empty seat in the house. Canute sat front and center, holding the Bible upside down, cooing like a wood pigeon, but for whatever the one-eyed idiot's faults he'd somehow managed to bring the entire town together with his newfound enthusiasm for Christ.

Father Thomas praised God and in turn was struck by divine inspiration. To celebrate this unexpected turn of events he would direct the villagers in a Passion play, for what better way to solidify their conversion than a dramatic rendering of Christ's last horrific hours? He filled out most of the apostles with fishermen and farmers and was surprised by Halvdan, who asked if he could share the part of Judas with his dog. Eirik grunted when assigned the role of Pontius Pilate, and Sigrid, who took eagerly to the role of Mary Magdalene, smiled boldly at the priest when he called her name. When Thomas reached the most important role of the play, he had but one name left on his list.

"Canute, the Lord may not have gifted you with a fully functional brain but by God He gave you a wonderfully big heart, and if that's not enough to play the biggest-hearted man who ever lived then I don't know what would be."

And here the old idiot stood and waddled to the pulpit where he looked at Thomas with an eye brimming with stupid emotion. He embraced the priest in a firm, cabbage-smelling hug but when he pulled away he shook his head vigorously, placed a finger on Thomas's forehead, and said, "Jesus."

"Oh, no, I couldn't," Thomas said, but then Canute led the entire church in a rousing if not repetitive chant of Thomas's name until finally the priest had no choice but to relent. "Well, all right, if you insist!"

They spent the next week slowly acquiring the necessary props, including a heavy cross carpentered from the wood of an ash tree. On Sunday the entire town of Grimsby convened at the church, all of them dressed for their parts. Thomas, himself wearing a sensible white robe, was surprised to see Canute duck through the doorway wearing what appeared to be a completely authentic uniform of a first century Roman prefect, replete with a plumed helmet and sharpened gladius.

"I'm afraid we've already cast Pilate," Thomas said sadly, "but we could always use another soldier."

Canute smiled.

***

Eirik, as Pilate, condemned Thomas to death with little handwringing and without much hesitation. In fact, he seemed quite happy to slam his hammer-cum-gavel against the church pulpit. Thomas thought this strange, but no matter, the skies were clouding over and it looked like nasty weather was afoot. Better to get the whole thing done before the storms began.

Canute led him out of the church and escorted him roughly to the square where he found himself chained to the fountain. The idiot brayed several times, then took a whip from off his hip and snapped it smartly against the ground.

"Oh, good thinking," said Thomas. He then proceeded to yelp when Canute snapped the whip into his back. "Let's be careful with that now, Canute. It's hardly a toy."

"Shut up, Jew!" someone who'd been slacking in their Bible studies yelled.

The whip snapped against his back again. A high-pitched scream subsided into a low chuckle as the priest gasped, "I admire your enthusiasm, really, but do try not to actually…"

The whip snapped yet again. Canute, in addition to being surprisingly spry for an elderly man, was also surprisingly true of aim for a one-eyed imbecile.

"Goddamnit!" Thomas cried involuntarily, and the whole crowd, what had begun to cheer, now lapsed into stunned silence that soon yielded to a surge of frenetic whispers: "He broke character."—"Can he do that?"—"Should we take it from the top?"

But Halvdan, ever the improviser, stepped forward and shouted, "Blasphemer!"

And suddenly the crowd, taking his cue, pitched rocks of varying sizes at Thomas while bellowing, "Kill the agitator!"

The next thing Thomas knew he was being manhandled to the edge of a farmer's field where the cross lay waiting in the dirt. Surely this is just some misunderstanding, he thought, struggling alone to lift its weight while simultaneously cursing himself for neglecting to cast the Cyrenian. They're probably just caught up in the moment. Yes, that's it. Then Sigrid approached with a prickly crown of thorns she'd fashioned and fitted it over his head. Athwart the field he was then compelled, and the crowd followed. Halvdan's mutt nipping at his heels. Canute's whip whistling through the air. When they reached that distant hilltop Father Thomas had seen when he'd first arrived on the outskirts of Grimsby, Halvdan appeared with a handful of spikes, and Eirik, eager to help, came forward with his gavel-cum-hammer.

"Look, gentlemen, I don't wish to interrupt your fun, but…"

They laid him flat and drove the spikes through his wrists and his ankles, nailing him tightly to the cross. His agonized screams floated off the hilltop, across the field, the town, and out over the nearby estuary where perhaps a seagull or two screeched in sympathy, although it's just as likely they didn't screech at all, oblivious as they are to the sophisticated world of men. Then they set the cross upright. Thomas hung there, crucified, his hands and feet bleeding freely. He looked down at the townsfolk and, having caught sight of Canute, noted a sinister look about the idiot's face.

Something occurred to Thomas.

"Devil!" he cried. "He's the devil!"

"Oh, look at him, picking on poor old Canute like that!" said one man.

"He hasn't got a mean bone in his body!" said another as Canute flicked the whip and caught Thomas cleanly across the cheek.

"He's a horse fucker," a voice from the crowd called out, "just like the other one!"

"I seen him do it too," Eirik said in pidgin English.

Sigrid tapped Halvdan on the shoulder and whispered something in his ear.

"And poor Sigrid says it wasn't even consensual!"

"I seen him do it too."

"Shame on you," Halvdan said. "Trying to take our precious Sigrid away from us."

Thomas, sobbing wildly now, cried out, "You'll all burn for this, you bastards!"

"That's a nice way for Jesus to talk."

And soon the crowd, growing bored of the spectacle, and anyway it had begun to rain, dispersed back to the village. The only one left, besides Thomas, was Canute. He looked up at the crucified priest with a vague air of apology. Then he sprang forward and ascended the cross, climbing first the base and then, when he was within reach, used Thomas's legs to climb even further, ignoring the painful shrieks of protestation, until finally they were both at eye-level. He leaned in as if to plant a romantic peck on Thomas's cheek but instead sucked the priest's left eyeball out of its socket. Then, grabbing hold of the wet dangly thing, he dropped from the cross and landed on his feet, Thomas's detached eye-ball, severed of its optic nerve, in the palm of his hand. He stuffed it immediately into his empty ocular cavity with a happy squeal.

"Bless you, God!" he said, then ran off down the hill to catch up with the others.

"Father!" Thomas sobbed, his one-eyed face craned skyward. "Why did you forsake me?"

The dark clouds above wept and roiled with a long and unnatural death rattle, and from their churning bosom descended a flash of ethereal light that lit the hilltop and resounded with a booming explosion. The lesson Father Thomas learned that day, his final lesson, as his flesh fried and soldered and became as one with the ash, was: *never cast a liturgical drama with a people who've yet to embrace the theatre.*

***

The next day, in Lincoln, a letter addressed to the bishop arrived at St. Mary's. The bishop broke the seal and extracted a report:

> "*...while certainly eccentric and undoubtedly of pagan persuasion, the inhabitants of Grimsby are, in the esti-*

235

mation of this observer, so far afield from their blood-thirsty forebears as to be utterly incapable of the murder with which they've been so insensitively charged. It is, therefore, recommended that the High Sheriff widen the investigation to include itinerant workers, traveling minstrels of low moral standing, or perhaps, who knows, even the French monks at Covenham may warrant scrutiny. As to the conversion, progress has been slow but fruitful; with the fullness of time they will all of them surely come to accept Jesus exclusively into their beleaguered hearts. Furthermore, I think, as a little push in the right direction, I shall conduct their flourishing faith in a most beautiful rendition of Christ's Passion—may the angels weep.

God's obedient and ever faithful servant,
Fr. Thomas.

P.S. Request, incidentally, the immediate assistance of a doctor, as some strange degenerative disease seems endemic to the region; marked by horrible rashes, lesions, pustules most foul, and, when relieving the bladder, a rather disquieting burning sensation."

***

IN ACTUAL HISTORY

Grimsby, a town in North East Lincolnshire, England, has its beginnings in the late 9th century when it was founded by Danish Vikings who, following the Great Heathen Army's victories against the Anglo-Saxon Kingdoms, gave up sowing their wild oats, so to speak, and settled down to a peaceful life of fishing on the Humber estuary. Thanks to its remote location within the Danelaw, the next two centuries of almost constant

Anglo-Danish warfare left Grimsby mercifully un-scathed. The 11th century saw, in addition to Denmark becoming a Christianized country, the successful inva-sion of England by William the Conqueror and, subse-quently, the end of the Viking Age. A census ordered by William in 1086 found Grimsby home to one church and one priest, and although it's altogether un-likely that the populace at that time still clung to their old gods, the humble needs of the story must ulti-mately, in this and other instances (including, but cer-tainly not limited to, Danish bathing customs, the anachronistic presence of a more dramatic, less hymnal take on Passion plays, and the dubious existences of any and all persons named Todd), take precedence over the inconvenient tyranny of historical reality.

ABOUT JOSEPH SHARP

Joseph Sharp is a recent graduate from the University of North Texas, where he majored in History. He is the author of such unpublished works as *Wet Floor, No More: A Multivolume History of the Shower Curtain*, and *Ten Righteous Men: Celestial Bargaining for Beginners*. He lives in Dallas.

Joseph Sharp is one of the winners of the *Crusader Kings II* Short Story Contest 2014.

OTHER TITLES BY
PARADOX BOOKS

A Fall of Kings: A Crusader Kings II Novel

The Chronicles of Konstantinos:
A Crusader Kings II Narrative Guide

What If? The *Europa Universalis IV*
Anthology of Alternate History

One Land, One Faith, One Queen:
A Europa Universalis IV Narrative Guide

The Communist Campaign in Karelia:
A Hearts of Iron III Strategy Guide

War of the Vikings: The Official Game Guide

Berserker King: A War of the Vikings Novel

Blood in the Streets: A War of the Roses Novel

The Sword is Mightier: A War of the Roses Novel

The Great Mage Game: A Warlock 2 Novel

The Ninth Element: A Magicka Novel

The Dark Between the Stars: A Coriolis Novel

A Year with Minecraft: Behind the Scenes at Mojang